PRAISE FOR WORKS

"Rocket-boosted action, brilliant speculation, and the recreation of a horror out of the mythologic past, all seamlessly blend into a rollercoaster ride of suspense and adventure."
-- James Rollins, New York Times bestselling author of JAKE RANSOM AND THE SKULL KING'S SHADOW

"With THRESHOLD Jeremy Robinson goes pedal to the metal into very dark territory. Fast-paced, action-packed and wonderfully creepy! Highly recommended!"
--Jonathan Maberry, NY Times bestselling author of ROT & RUIN

"Jeremy Robinson is the next James Rollins"
-- Chris Kuzneski, NY Times bestselling author of THE SECRET CROWN

"If you like thrillers original, unpredictable and chock-full of action, you are going to love Jeremy Robinson..."
-- Stephen Coonts, NY Times bestselling author of DEEP BLACK: ARCTIC GOLD

"How do you find an original story idea in the crowded action-thriller genre? Two words: Jeremy Robinson."
-- Scott Sigler, NY Times Bestselling author of ANCESTOR

"There's nothing timid about Robinson as he drops his readers off the cliff without a parachute and somehow manages to catch us an inch or two from doom."
-- Jeff Long, New York Times bestselling author of THE DESCENT

THE LAST HUNTER

Ascent

(Book 3 of the Antarktos Saga)

JEREMY ROBINSON

BREAKNECK MEDIA

For the real Solomon, my son and inspiration

ACKNOWLEDGEMENTS.

I must once again thank a small group of people who make the Antarktos Saga some of the best books I've written. Kane Gilmour, your edits continue to improve my books, and as you've come to know my stories better than anyone else, your guidance and opinions are invaluable. Stan Tremblay, you not only continue to support my books, but you took over the formatting of ASCENT with flawless precision. My wife, Hilaree, and my two girls, Aquila and Norah, your creativity and energy keeps this family imagining. And Solomon, my son, upon whom The Last Hunter is based... When I began this series, I wondered if the attributes you possessed as a three year old—kindness, gentleness, forgiveness—would remain as you aged. You're now five and still a better example of these things than anyone I've ever known. Thank you.

FICTION BY JEREMY ROBINSON

The Antarktos Saga
The Last Hunter - Pursuit
The Last Hunter - Descent
The Last Hunter - Ascent

The Jack Sigler Thrillers
Threshold
Instinct
Pulse
Callsign: King - Book 1
Callsign: Queen - Book 1
Callsign: Rook - Book 1
Callsign: Knight - Book 1
Callsign: Bishop - Book 1
Callsign: King - Book 2 - Underworld

Origins Editions (first five novels)
Kronos
Antarktos Rising
Beneath
Raising the Past
The Didymus Contingency

Writing as Jeremy Bishop
Torment
The Sentinel

Short Stories
Insomnia

Humor
The Zombie's Way (Ike Onsoomyu)
The Ninja's Path (Kutyuso Deep)

THE LAST HUNTER

PROLOGUE

Lieutenant Ninnis looked at the blade in his hand. The bright sun overhead reflected off its surface, the intensity of its gleam burning his eyes. But the pain didn't bother him. Not because it was insignificant—even after spending nearly three months above ground, the sunlight still hurt his eyes—but because the pain delighted him.

Delighted Nephil.

The body and spirit of Nephil that resided in his body had been meant for another. Solomon Ull Vincent. A boy. The first and only child naturally born of a human being on the continent of Antarctica. The child bonded with the land on a supernatural level. Beyond understanding.

And now, beyond reach.

Ninnis turned his eyes away from the blade, and looked at the soft earth beneath his bare feet. His soles had become so thick with calluses from living underground that he couldn't feel the softness of the fresh leaf litter. But it smelled raw. Alive. He'd always believed that subterranean life was ideal. He'd never understood why the Nephilim—the half human, half demon ancients he once called masters—obsessed about taking the surface back from the human race. But after spending the last week feeling the burn of the sun, moving through the young forest and hunting in a way that's impossible underground, Ninnis understood.

The surface is wide open. Limitless.

And beautiful.

He didn't admire sunsets, flowers or the glimmering ocean that now filled the previously frozen bay to the north. He didn't watch the butterflies or birds that now filled the warm Antarctic air. He didn't marvel at the herds of underworld creatures adapting to life under the sun. None of this interested him.

A twitch brought his attention back to the man at his feet.

Blood flowed through the man's fingers and mixed with the soil. Hungry worms rose to the surface, feasting on the blood. Drowning in it. This is what Ninnis liked about the surface. The color.

Life underground was muted by darkness. Even when lit by torches, glowing crystals or the large electric bulbs in the Nephilim libraries, the world underground looked dull. But here, in the light, vivid colors danced with every shift of the breeze. And the blood—*the blood*—it glistened with the most delicious hue of dark red. The sight of it delighted him almost as much as the smell.

A tattoo of swirling spikes covered the large, bald man's head. Ninnis wasn't sure if they represented anything, but he was positive they were meant to intimidate. Covered with a splash of the man's own blood, they looked silly. He wore black clothing from the neck down and much of his face had been painted black. At night, or underground, the man would be hard to see. But in the light, reeking of sweat, the man stood out like a beacon. He carried two knives, a handgun and a long black rifle Ninnis had never seen, but recognized as a sharpshooter's rifle.

A soldier.

A hunter.

Ninnis chuckled at the thought.

Defeating this man had been no more difficult than defeating a newborn feeder. The man bore sharp blades, moved quickly and struck hard, but he lacked knowledge about the true world around him. Seeing Ninnis dressed in nothing more than tattered leathers had actually made the soldier laugh. The man mocked him in Russian before realizing Ninnis didn't speak the language, and then switched to English. Ninnis showed no reaction to the man's taunts. Instead, he circled the man, gauging this newcomer to *his* land.

They race to claim my continent, Ninnis had thought, *only to find it already taken.*

Fools.

When Strike appeared in Ninnis's hands, the shocked expression on the man's face was comical. And as the soldier fumbled to draw his pistol, Ninnis closed the distance, and eviscerated the man.

He now lay on the ground, clutching his belly to keep his insides from sliding out. Two seconds and one strike. The man had faced a god, and lost. As did anyone, or anything, that stood up to Ninnis. As the vessel of Nephil, he commanded the subterranean armies. More than that, he had the devotion of creatures that have lived for thousands of years before he was born, before he was taken captive in 1911 and turned into Ninnis the hunter, subject to Enki, son of Nephil. And now Enki, who along with his brother Enlil, previously ruled over the Nephilim, served *him*. They didn't realize this, of course. He contained the physical body and spirit of Nephil, who'd been imprisoned in Tartarus and recently freed. The ancient spirit possessed unimaginable power, but it couldn't control Ninnis. Instead, he decided to take the power for himself and use it to lead the Nephilim to victory over the surface world. While his goals aligned with those of the Nephilim, he would age more quickly on the surface. Death would claim him eventually. To obtain immortality, he would wipe out humanity quickly, and become legend, remembered for eternity as the savior of the Nephilim.

He could feel the power eating at him from the inside out. Eventually, the spirit of Nephil would be released, most likely upon Ninnis's deathbed. Without the boy, Solomon, willingly offering himself to Nephil, the spirit would die. And there is nothing Nephilim feared more than death. Within the realm of Tartarus, the spirit of Nephil had existed in a state of eternal torture beyond comprehension. It was a place designed to contain and punish the Nephilim, who had so long ago corrupted mankind before being chased underground and buried beneath Antarctica's ice cap. Outside of Tartarus, if a Nephilim died, they simply ceased to exist. Their spirits were different from human souls. They lacked something, some kind of substance, and would simply fade away.

Ull, the Nephilim who had shared Solomon's middle name and become his master, had suffered such a fate after the boy killed him. No hunters other than Ninnis and Kainda knew about his fate, but...

Kainda.

Remembering his daughter brought a glimmer of discomfort to his chest. It was a kind of pain in which he did not delight. Because he didn't understand it. She betrayed him. Left with the boy, Luca, and his sister, Emilie—traitors all three. They were why he now stalked the freshly grown wilderness. Preparations to invade the outside world would continue in his absence. He didn't foresee humanity putting up much of a struggle. They had been devastated by the massive shift in the Earth's crust that had repositioned Antarctica at the equator and returned the land to the lush paradise it had been so long ago.

But paradise would be stained with blood. First, the man at his feet. Then any other outsiders foolish enough to try to claim Antarctica. And finally, Kainda and the thirty-six other hunters who deserted the underground and their masters. Only after he'd seen the life drain from their bodies would he give the signal to attack the rest of the world.

A sudden scratch of shifting leaves snapped Ninnis out of his thoughts. The soldier showed resolve. The man drew a blade from a sheath on his chest and sent it flying toward Ninnis, who did nothing to avoid it.

Four inches of steel pierced Ninnis's chest and slipped between his ribs, puncturing a lung. The intense pain would have knocked any other man to his knees.

Ninnis smiled.

Holding his gut with one hand, the man pushed himself away from Ninnis.

Ninnis twitched his wrist and Strike's blade rolled up. He attached the weapon to his belt, and looked down at the hilt of the knife sticking out of his chest. An expert shot. The man might have made a good hunter after all. But Ninnis no longer had any interest in breaking and making hunters. Solomon had been the last hunter, destined to contain the spirit of Nephil, and that hadn't turned out as planned. Once the Nephilim reclaimed the surface, there would be no need for hunters, whose small bodies made them important assets in the underworld.

Ninnis clutched the knife in his chest and drew it out slowly. An explosion of pain radiated through his body. The blade came free with a slurp. Blood followed.

Purple blood.

Ninnis watched the violet plasma drip down his chest, fascinated by its color. Human blood—his blood—ran red. He'd been carrying a feeder skin of Nephilim blood, consuming it regularly so that its healing properties could help his human body endure the rigors of containing Nephil. It would also have no trouble healing this wound. But would it have to? Ninnis watched as the flow of blood slowed, and then stopped.

An intense itch surrounded the wound and then pulsed with pain. It felt like being stabbed all over again, but in reverse. And then, the wound was healed.

Ninnis knew he was changing. He felt hungrier. More ruthless.

More powerful. More hard-hearted. But he hadn't realized the changes were also *physical*.

"I am becoming Nephilim," he said.

The soldier at his feet continued to struggle, a pitiful whimper escaping his mouth. Ninnis looked the man in the eyes. "I'm changing," he said. "And hungry."

Ninnis brought the soldier's razor sharp knife up to his eyes and looked at his reflection through the smear of his own purple blood. He licked the blade clean, and smiled at the man. "My appetite seems to have changed." He cocked his head to the side. "I hope you don't find it rude if I make you watch while I eat."

The man filled his lungs to scream as Ninnis lunged toward him.

And ate.

1

I'm cold.

The thought has repeated itself in my mind a thousand times before I think to do something about it. It's been so long since I had to worry about hot and cold, that I'm confused by the sensation. While I remember a variety of ways to remedy the situation, my body has lost the instinct. My teeth aren't chattering. I don't rub my arms, or hop up and down. I just...stand. And wait. For something. I don't know what.

For it to end, I think. *This nightmare.*

I stand before the black gates of Tartarus, staring into the light absorbing darkness, hoping they'll open again. I haven't moved since I stepped inside, though I have replayed that fateful decision in between each and every, 'I'm cold'.

The Nephilim had me surrounded. Ninnis, possessed by the body and spirit of Nephil, stood before me. Powerful. Strong enough to take me. Maybe even break me. And that is a fate that neither I, nor the world, would like to see realized.

It would mean the end of all things.

Though I suspect the world might be doomed, anyway. If anyone could have challenged Nephil, it was me. I know that now. It took help, but I repelled Nephil from my mind and my body, and in a very real way, I defeated the powerful first Nephilim. It wasn't the first time Nephil had tasted defeat, of course. Someone put him here, in Tartarus, to begin with.

My hope, my only hope, is that someone on the outside knows how to get me out the same way Nephil got out. I'm certain no one outside of the Nephilim inner circle—Enki, Enlil, Odin, Thor, Zeus and the other ancient gods—has a clue, though. So my hope's eternal flame is more of a pitiful flicker. At best.

I realize I've been staring at the doors for some time now. How long, I really have no idea. Time seems irrelevant here. I could have been here a few seconds or a thousand years. I'm not sure. My world currently consists of the ground beneath my feet, the big black doors standing in front of me and the ever-biting cold that has now reached my bones.

Turn around, I tell myself.

But I can't.

I'm terrified by what I might see, not because I know what it is, but because I have no clue. Tartarus is a land of eternal punishment, created expressly for the punishment of Nephilim. The *Nephilim*! They're giants that delight in pain and heal instantaneously. Saying, "You want to go torture each other?" to a Nephilim is like if my friend Justin asked me to spend the night at the Museum of Science in Boston.

So how am I supposed to endure something the Nephilim find torturous?

I'm not.

I'm going to stand right here until the end of time and wait for this door to open.

Several minutes, or maybe years, later, my eyes drift. I see stone. Bleak, pale stone. But at least it's recognizable. It's something I can comprehend. Maybe this place isn't as otherworldly as I expected.

A tick of stone on stone snaps my head to the side. The small pebble rolls and stops at my feet. The bitter sting of a breeze eats away at my back. I catch a glimpse of the barren, rocky world behind me, and turn forward as the wind cuts into my face and whips through my hair.

I should be dead, I realize. Hypothermic at the very least. I look at my fingers, expecting to see the onset of frostbite. My hands look normal. They just hurt.

Without a conscious decision to do so, I turn around. I'm at the bottom of a short stone hill. Average looking rocks cover the surface. If not for the swirling orange sky, the landscape, as far as I can see it, could be mistaken for the American southwest. *Utah*, I think. *It looks like Arches National Monument.*

Despite the cold, there is no snow. No moisture in the air at all, actually.

Thinking of water makes me thirsty. More thirsty than I thought possible. The sensation moves me forward, up the rise. As I move away from the door, I take in my surroundings. I can't see far. More rocky terrain rises up to my left and right. And the gates of Tartarus are so large behind me that I can't yet see around them.

A burst of frigid wind slams into my face as I clear the top of the rise. I push against the wind with my thoughts, but it's no use. My link to the continent is gone. Unless, I realize, I am no longer on Antarctica. *This is some kind of supernatural realm or alternate dimension*, I think. It's a ridiculous thought. Before returning to Antarctica, being kidnapped, broken and turned into Ull the hunter, I was a bookworm in love with science. There isn't a single theory in the books I read that make a place like this possible.

Of course, they wouldn't make sense of the Nephilim either and I have long since given up wondering how half-human, half-demons are even possible, never mind the supernatural forces that gave birth to them.

I wipe the wind-born tears from my eyes, tilt my head away from the wind and step over the top of the hill. The bitter wind tugs at my feeble clothing—just a belt and a Tarzan-like leather loincloth—and I realize I still have all of my belongings. Whips-nap is attached to my waist, though I don't remember putting it there. I have a knife, telescope, sunglasses and a flint stone for starting fires—not that there is anything flammable here. In subterranean Antarctica, I would have used dried dung to create a fire. Here, in this barren place, I don't even have that foul resource.

The wind dies suddenly, as though finally accepting my presence. When I look up, I don't see fire and brimstone. There's nothing inherently Biblical or hellish about the place. An endless expanse of barren hills and gorges laid out beneath an angry orange sky. I can't see any sun to speak of. This could be another planet. It could be underground. Or it could be something beyond my understanding.

I crane my head side to side and see nothing. Endless nothing. A deep sense of loneliness twists around inside me and makes a nice spot for itself in my gut. A shiver rises from my legs and shakes through my core. My body, it seems, has just remembered how it's supposed to respond to freezing. My muscles twitch so hard I find it difficult to stand.

What's the point of standing? I think.

There is no place to go. Despite the cold, I'm not going to die. In fact, I might already be dead. So I should probably just sit down, grit my teeth and wait for eternity to end.

A moment later, I shake so bad that I don't have a choice. I fall down to my butt and pull my legs in close. But there is no escaping the cold. Nor the loneliness. This is the fate I chose when I stepped back into the gates of Tartarus. This is the sacrifice I made to save Luca. As I begin to weep, a shift in the orange sky at the horizon catches my attention.

There's something there. Something different from the endless rolling stone hills and swirling sky. It's sharp. And vertical. *A tower*, I realize.

I stay rooted in place. In this place, the tower can't be a good thing.

But it's something.

Where's Ull? I wonder. Ull is my middle name, given to me by

Dr. Merrill Clark, a friend of my parents, husband of Aimee Clark, whom I kidnapped and delivered to the Nephilim, and the father of Mirabelle Clark, the first girl I had any kind of romantic feeling for. But Ull became my one and only name after I was broken by Ninnis and turned into a hunter. I served the Nephilim Ull, son of Thor, before killing him, too. But 'Ull' is now how I identify that dark side of me—the side that enjoyed being a hunter. He is part of me, but also separate from me. In fact, we generally loath each other, though we worked together to force Nephil from my—*our*—mind. But I have yet to sense his ferocity, his strength. I fear that aspect of my personality has either been suppressed or removed. Ull's passion would help me now, and I suspect helping someone, even a split personality, might be against the rules of this place.

With shaking hands, I dig into one of my pouches and take out the telescope given to me by Ninnis on my birthday, back when I was still Ull. I fight to extend the frozen metal as it clings to my skin. But I get it open and peek through the lens, careful not to let my eyeball touch, and flash freeze to, the metal. The tower comes into view, still distant, but clearer. It's not natural, I think. Someone built it. But why? And when? And for what purpose?

Where Ull is passionate, I am curious. And in this case, the resulting action is the same. I push myself up against the cold and set out toward the tall tower. I could probably figure out how far away it is, but have no need to figure out how long the journey will take.

I have eternity.

2

I wish I could say, "I can't remember the last time I felt this desperate for warmth." But I can't say it. I remember *everything*. The last time I should have felt cold was a few years ago when I first climbed down the airplane stairs and stepped onto the Antarctic ice. I wore only pants and a long sleeve shirt. The cold should have stung me then, like it does now. But I felt nothing. Immunity to the temperature on, and under, Antarctica was the first manifestation of my connection to the continent. For the past several years, I've experienced the elements somewhere around seventy-five degrees, night or day, covered in snow or standing in a fire pit.

But now...

A shudder quakes through my body.

I push through it, walking in what I hope is a straight line, toward the distant tower now hidden by the rising grade before me.

As I walk up, I search my memories for warmth. Before coming to Antarctica, I was a cartoon junkie. At least, I was on

Saturday morning, when the good cartoons were on. But it's not the shows I focus on. It's my afghan. My mother knitted the rainbow colored blanket for me and it rested at the end of my bed, every night of my life. My father turned down the heat at night, which left the downstairs bitterly cold on winter mornings in Maine. So the afghan found its way around my shoulders most winter mornings and warmed me while I ate my cereal, watched cartoons and drew.

The memory warms my heart, but does little to improve my physical condition. I've heard that just thinking about fire can warm your body, but I'm now positive that's a bunch of malarkey.

Malarkey. Justin's mother used that word a lot. Mostly when we'd done something awful (like leave a scuffmark in the pristine, forbidden living room). We were always full of malarkey back then.

I trip and fall to my hands and knees. I hit hard, but feel no pain. I'm too numb to feel it. When I look up, I realize my reverie had done its job distracting me. The hill is gone. I'm in a gorge, but I have no memory of cresting the hill, descending the other side or entering this valley. I look back and the stone walls wrap around a corner, obscuring my view of whatever terrain I covered to get here.

The dream-like quality of my arrival in this new place disturbs me, but there's no wind here. I'm also somewhat comforted by the stripes of stone strata surrounding me. If not for the strip of orange sky thirty feet above me, this would feel like the underground, which, if I'm honest, has become my home.

I search the area for a cave, or even a good-sized crack I can squeeze into. If there is an underground here, maybe I could warm up. The ambient temperature just ten feet underground is fifty-five degrees. Not exactly warm, but it's an improvement. Survivable. Not that I'm dying. I don't think it's possible to die in Tartarus. What good would an eternal land of torment be if you could simply die to escape?

I can't see the tower anymore. The gorge might lead me in the wrong direction, but going back doesn't appeal to me. My bare feet slap on the smooth stone floor as I begin walking forward once more. The smoothness of the stone tells me that a stream once ran through here and eroded rock. Which means that there could be water.

Ice, more like it, I think. But I could melt it.

Thinking about water kick starts my stomach again. I fish into a pouch and pull out a dry stick of meat. It's tough, and I need to grind my teeth to eat it, but the two bites I ration for myself feel like a Thanksgiving dinner.

Images of Thanksgivings past rocket through my mind. I hear family laughing and telling stories. I smell the turkey cooking. My mouth waters as it remembers the tangy sweetness of mom's homemade cranberry sauce.

In a flash, the two bites of dried flesh seem entirely inadequate. My stomach shouts for more. I'm tempted to consume all of my meager food supply, but life in the underground has taught me discipline. I turn my thoughts away from food.

I look up and find the gorge transformed. I've lost myself again. It doesn't look like I've gone as far this time, but who's to say this gorge isn't a hundred miles long. Not that time has any meaning here. I could have just walked for a year. A hundred years. The Nephilim might have already taken over the planet. Luca, Em, Aimee and Mira might all be dead and buried. Maybe there isn't even a human race to return to?

Could this be the torture of Tartarus? Not knowing? Have I been here for ten minutes? Or ten years? I feel my face, expecting to find the long shaggy beard of an older man. But there's nothing. Not even the quarter inch of fuzz that had grown on my cheeks. My skin is smooth. Soft even.

I look at my arms. They're thin and frail. *Like I was before life underground.* The arms of a nerd. *What's happened to me?*

Weakness, I think.

This place is searching for my weakness. I'm unaccustomed to the cold, so it freezes me. My memories hurt more than help. And now my physical strength has been taken. *One at a time*, I think. This place is going to whittle away at me, bit by bit, until I'm so pitiful that I wish for death. Which, of course, will never come. The process won't be quick, either. There's plenty of time.

How would this play out for a Nephilim? Pain would hurt. Really hurt. They would be vulnerable. Frail. Small. Helpless.

Like me.

Like the real me.

Pitiful.

To be pitied.

My thoughts turn down a dark road of self-loathing and I'm not going to stop it. I deserve this. I asked for this.

As my attention shifts inward once again, I lose sight of the stone walls around me. The world slips away.

For a moment.

And then it returns with a sharp impact.

I stumble back, hand to head, confused by what's happened. The tunnel turned and I didn't turn with it. I walked straight into the wall.

Klutz.

The sharp pain brings tears to my eyes.

Crybaby.

The voice in my head reminds me of Ull, but it's not him. It's me. Or this place. I can't tell the difference, but wherever it comes from, it knows exactly what to say.

"Shut up!" I shout. My voice echoes through the crevasse. To punctuate my anger, I make a fist and swing a punch toward my own leg. But the pain of the blow is dull. At first I think it's because my body has become so frail, lacking the strength even to inflict pain on itself. But that's not it. I punched something.

Something solid. But not like a rock, or it would have hurt my hand.

I look at the pouch hanging off the right side of my belt. Something large and rectangular fills it. After untying the leather strap holding it shut, I flip the pouch open and gasp.

It's a book.

A book.

My memory of the thing returns. I took it from the Nephilim library in Asgard, when I returned to see Aimee, before heading for the gates of Tartarus. I pull the brown leather-bound book out of the pouch, and I look at the faded gold text on the spine.

Despite the tortures of this place, I smile, and read the text on the front cover.

The Pilgrim's Progrefs
John Bunyan

I note that the title is spelled with an "fs" at the end, which was common in the sixteen hundreds. This is an old copy, I think, and I gently open the cover.

THE
Pilgrim's Progrefs
FROM
THIS WORLD,
TO
That which is to come:
Delivered under the Similitude of a
DREAM
Wherein is Difcovered,
The manner of his letting out,
His Dangerous Journey; And fafe
Arrival at the Defired Countrey.
By *John Bunyan*
LONDON,
Printed for *Nath. Ponder* at the *Peacock*
in the *Poultrey* near *Cornhil*, 1678.

1678... 1678! This is a first edition, I think, growing excited.

Before coming to Antarctica, reading books was a passion of mine. My parents had thousands. I read them all and then some. I consumed them. But not this one. I've *never* read this book. I turn the page and read.

The AUTHOR'S *Apology* For His BOOK
When at the first I took my Pen in hand,
Thus for to write; I did not understand
That I at all should make a little Book
In such a mode; Nay, I had undertook
To make another, which, when almost done,
Before I was aware, I this begun.

By the time I reach that seventh line, I've forgotten the tower. The cold. The pain. And my feeble condition. The horrible world I now live in slips away as these words, written more than three hundred years ago, reach out across time, and maybe space, and deliver a gift I thought impossible in this place.

Hope.

3

I read each word slowly and with deliberation, as though I've just learned the language. The old English text is rich in a way that modern books aren't. I reread most sentences two or three times, just enjoying the cadence of the words. The plight of the main character, Christian, whose story is an allegory to the modern believer's life, fascinates me as many elements reflect my own journey over the past years. He's plagued by doubt, fear and the heavy burden that comes from the recognition of your own sins.

My sins weigh on me every day, impossible to forget thanks to my perfect memory.

I kidnapped Aimee and delivered her to the Nephilim, robbing Mira of a mother and Merrill of a wife.

I fled the Nephilim for what I thought was two years, but it turned out to be twenty. I hid in fear and turned my back on the world I was uniquely suited to defend.

Because of my weakness, Tobias, father of Emilie and Luca, was slain at the hands of Ninnis, while I watched, helpless.

And most recently, when I contained the body and spirit of Nephil, I fear he was able to affect the world somehow. Any devastation caused by my inability to fight his influence is mine to own.

My burden, like Christian's, is often unbearable. Even more so, in this awful place. If not for this book, and the distraction provided by it, I might have already gone mad. I've read the book now, cover to cover, several times. I'm not sure how long I've been sitting in the gorge, slowly turning pages, absorbing the words, but if I can just stay here, reading this book, I might be able to bear this place.

"Sorry Christian," I say to myself, "but you're going to have to share my burden, too."

Then it happens. I reach the chapter that has tickled the back of my mind on every read.

The Slough of Despond.

Thus far, I've read through it quickly, ignoring the potent message and similarities to my current situation. But something clicks as I read through the text this time:

This miry slough is such a place as cannot be mended: it is the descent whither the scum and filth that attends conviction for sin doth continually run, and therefore it is called the Slough of Despond; for still, as the sinner is awakened about his lost condition, there arise in his soul many fears and doubts, and discouraging apprehensions, which all of them get together, and settle in this place: and this is the reason of the badness of this ground.

"I'm in the slough," I say. My voice sounds deeper then I recall, but I think it's from thirst and the echo of my voice on the crevasse walls.

The Slough of Despond, which essentially means, the Swamp of Despair, in Bunyan's story seems to identify the burdens of the traveler stuck in the mire. In my case, the swamp is a dry wasteland, cut off from the rest of the world. But the effects of the place, like the Slough, focuses on the fears, weaknesses and burden of those unfortunate enough to be here. And the effect seems to increase with time, even if time makes no sense. If not for the book and its story of redemption...

My eyes are drawn back to the page. I don't want to read this section again. Despite the similarities to my stay in Tartarus, it is actually ruining my hope. Not because it ends badly, but because Christian is eventually pulled from the Slough by the aptly named, Help.

Despite being stuck in the Slough of Despond, Christian still inhabits the real world, and while one friend abandons him in the mire, another comes along to pull him out. But here, cut off from everyone and everything, there will be no travelers coming along to lend me aid. I'm alone. Forever. And even if I do eventually move from my spot in the gorge, the only living thing I have any hope of finding in this place is a Nephilim. I'm not sure how many are here, if any, but I don't think Nephil was alone in this place. And finding a Nephilim, in Tartarus, is not high on my eternal "to do" list.

I close the book, its words now adding to my burden. *Maybe it's Tartarus?* I think. At first, the book provided a distraction from the power of this place, but even the words of this book couldn't hold off Tartarus forever.

I look up and stare at the blank wall in front of me.

Whispered taunts flow past my ears.

You killed me.

The voice belongs to Tobias.

Emilie hates you.

I clench my eyes shut, trying to ignore a voice I know I can't be hearing. *Tobias is dead*, I remind myself. *He can't speak to me.*

Where do you think you are, Solomon? Alive?

"Stop," I say. "You're not him."

Luca is dead.

"Stop."

It's a lie.

Murdered.

"Please."

Luca escaped.

Because of you.

If there were fluid in my body to spare, tears would cover my cheeks. Tobias's voice brings back a torrent of memories. The day we met, he and Em nearly killed me. But we became friends. We became family. I lived with them for a time, becoming a brother to Em and to Luca, whose six year old body was a perfect copy of mine, created by the Nephilim. We ate together. We hunted together. And Tobias trained me. I learned to use my powers more effectively. More efficiently. And he taught me to get back up. To fight. To win.

And right now, I'm losing.

This isn't the voice of Tobias, but if it were, he would be ashamed of how I'm handling myself.

I replay a memory, tuning out the false-Tobias.

I'm running. The crunch of snow beneath my feet makes counting my footfalls easy: nine thousand, five hundred, and fifty-seven steps. Nearly five miles. I can run further. A lot further. And at a faster pace. But not while controlling the elements around me. Tobias has me running, cloaked by a swirling cyclone of snow.

We started with a single flake. It trailed me as I ran. Over time, we worked up to a trail of snowflakes. And when I'd mastered that, we moved to this. I think it's a big leap ahead. My body certainly agrees. Not only do I need to create thousands of snowflakes, I also need to sustain a steady, and tightly controlled wind around my body. I managed okay for the first mile. But it's been getting harder with each step.

To make matters worse, I can't see where I'm going. Every hundred steps, I open a slice in the cyclone and peek out. The added effort hurts every time, but the terrain has been unceasingly flat and free of debris since we began. So when I hit nine thousand six hundred, I don't look.

Ten seconds later, my foot kicks a spire of ice that I would have seen if I'd looked. I collapse forward in an embarrassing heap. I don't even bother to raise my hands. I just slump to the ice like a freed marionette and slide to a stop.

Tobias is a gentle man for the most part, but not when training. And he's pushing me hard, with an urgency that in hindsight makes me wonder if he knew his life would be cut short. He stands over me, shouting with a German accent that makes his words sound even angrier. "Get up! Get up, now, Solomon! Your life depends on it."

Concern for my own well-being isn't usually what garners a response from me. And Tobias knows this. So he quickly switches tactics. "They're coming, Solomon. They've found us!"

I'm listening, but I'm still far from moving. "They've found them. Em and Luca. If you don't get up—" He doesn't need to finish. I'm up and running, concealed by the cyclone, but this time I sustain the opening and double my pace. I'm not doing this for me. I'm doing this for them. For Em. For Luca. For Aimee.

And for Tobias.

Get up!

I chose to be here.

Get up, Solomon!

For them.

"I'm up," I say.

I look to my right, and then to the left. Left, I think. That's where I was headed. As the biting chill, held at bay by the book's distraction, settles in around me, I put my book away, turn left, and run.

4

I grow tired almost immediately. But I focus on the true voice of Tobias, urging me onward, and I push forward. My effort must be considered a crime in this place, because the weight on my shoulders becomes palpable. I can feel something—a force— pushing down on me. Holding me back. Like I'm in a dream.

Maybe that's it, I think. *Maybe this is all a dream?*

In a strange sort of way, it would make sense. After passing through the gate, into the darkness, the traveler falls asleep. Then maybe someone, some kind of caretaker, drags your sleeping body deeper underground where aging is slowed so much it's actually stopped. And then, in the pliable world of the sleeping mind, the prisoner is forced to grapple with his own self-doubt, fears and weakness. This place is barren. All stone and orange sky. My mind could have easily conjured the image.

And if this is all in my mind, I can control it. I once read about something called "lucid dreaming." Essentially, the drea- mer recognizes they're dreaming and then controls the dream, bending it to their will. People routinely realize they're in a dream, but typically wake very quickly when they do. Lucid dreamers use various techniques to stay in the dream. Dream spinning (spinning in circles) or physical contact—rubbing your hands together or touching the ground—supposedly work well.

But I've also learned to control the reality my mind creates thanks to Xin. So, I should be able to manage it here.

I pause my running. Each labored breath accentuates the cramp twisting in my side.

It certainly feels physical.

But dreams can, too. So I focus on the world around me and try to change it.

Nothing happens.

Wait, I think. *I'm warmer.* Then I realize that I only feel slightly warmer from running. Everything else is the same. Can't say I'm surprised. This might all be in my mind, but inside Tartarus, whatever it is, I can't control things. And I can't wake up.

The angry weight settles heavier. It strikes so suddenly that I pitch forward. I catch myself against the wall of the gorge. My foot lands hard, but not on solid stone.

There is a squishing sound as something lukewarm oozes up between my bare toes. The mush gives way to something hard and splintery. I feel, more than hear, the tiny things snap under my weight. All of this happens in a fraction of a second. Before I've put all of my weight down, I flinch back, and fall over.

The gravity inside Tartarus seems to increase suddenly. I fall hard, harder than I should from a standing position. And my body lacks the strength to slow me down. I hit the stone floor hard, knocking the air from my lungs. I wheeze and for a moment, I fear I won't be able to catch my breath.

I can't die, I tell myself. Relax. Breathe. Focus.

My chest expands a little more with each breath and my thoughts clear. My foot is wet. I stepped in something. After looking at my elbows for wounds and finding none, I push myself up and draw my foot in close. There is a smear of thick red fluid on the sole.

Blood.

But it's not mine. There's too much and I don't see a wound.

Well, that's not entirely true. There seems to be a large splinter of something jabbed between my first and second toes. It's a small, curved spear of white. I take hold of it and tug gently. The inch long splinter slides cleanly out. A bead of blood emerges from the wound, but that's it. I can't even feel the sting. I'm far too cold for that.

I look at the spine up close. Is it a quill? *No*, I think, *it's not barbed.* Images of high school science books and dissection diagrams come to mind. It looks like a rib. Like a mouse rib.

Curiosity pulls me up onto my hands and knees. I lean forward searching for the spot where my foot fell.

It's not hard to find.

The small body is surrounded by a syrupy pool of blood and other, oddly colored bodily fluids. As for the creature, I can't say what it is. Or was. It's been brutalized. Torn to pieces. And it looks like the whole thing is here. Four legs. Two small arms. It must have walked like an insect, but also had functional arms. The skin is green, and slick with slime, like a frog.

The torso looks like it was torn open, not cut, and the skin has been peeled back. The organs are gone. I find them splattered against the wall nearby, glued to the surface by the drying fluids. The exposed ribcage has been snapped open on either side, the small spiked ends pointing skyward. One rib is missing.

I look at the small rib clutched between my fingers, then toss it down on the ground and turn my attention back to the mutilated corpse. The lungs, like the other organs, have been torn out. They rest on the cavern floor nearby. When I see the heart, I have no doubt that whatever did this was evil. The grape-sized heart rests in the center of the exposed ribs, still attached to the body by several arteries. But the organ has been crushed, and burst open.

This creature did not die peacefully.

I have killed small creatures in the past. If I had come across it living, I would have killed it now. But for food. And swiftly. Not like this. This was…

Torture.

But why? This small thing couldn't be a Nephilim.

A realization strikes. This is real. This creature, the likes of which I have never seen before, once lived. And was killed by something else living. Something other than me.

This is not a dream, I think as I stand up. I wring my hands together and begin to shiver, as much from fear as from the cold.

I'm not alone.

And whatever else lurks in this gorge with me, likes to torture things.

But I'm not defenseless. I place a hand on Whipsnap. Its

presence reassures me. But my withered body betrays me. Could I even lift Whipsnap? I don't think so. *Be prepared*, I think, quoting the Boy Scouts jingle I grew up with. The tune plays in my thoughts.

Are you ready to get involved?

Be prepared! Are you ready to take the lead?

"No, and no," I say.

But what choice do I have? I'm here. I'm stuck here. Forever. So what's the point in going the other way? I might be physically weaker, but I'm not a coward. Not any more. I've faced my fears before. I can do it now.

I reach into my hip pack and take out my climbing claws. I created them myself, fashioning them from feeder leather and teeth. The big triangular teeth are serrated, like sharks' teeth, and they can cut through most any flesh with ease. They're based on the ninja climbing claws in Justin's old ninja magazines, but these are more functional as weapons. When I slide them on my hands and cinch them tight, I've got three triangular blades on the palm side, but I also have three more spiky blades over my knuckles. My hands are now lethal. And they don't weigh much, so even in my weakened state I should be able to use them.

When I step out into the gorge and look down the winding tunnel, I'm not so sure.

Ten feet further is a second body. Like the first, it has been mutilated beyond recognition.

Beyond that is another.

And another.

The trail of blood and guts covers nearly a hundred feet before disappearing around a bend. I step forward, careful to avoid the blood and organs littering the floor. It's slow going, but at least the sight of carnage and the smells of new decay distract me from the chill. A surge of guilt strikes me. What an awful thing to think. I look down at the small body. Still… "At least you found a way out," I say to the creature.

I round the bend and find another passage littered with death. Growing accustomed to the sight, I quicken my pace. The wind has picked up, and I think I must be nearing the end of the chasm. Bright light stretches into the natural hall around a bend fifty feet ahead. I hurry forward, now eager to escape this place.

A wet cracking and slurping sound whips my head up. Not watching where I'm going, I step on a small set of lungs that turn to paste beneath my weight. I slip back and fall again.

The pain is intense, but I don't cry out.

A wet splat, followed by an agonized howl, rolls down the gorge.

I've found him.

The torturer.

He's just ahead.

I pick myself up without making a sound and slip toward the bend. All I need is a peek. If it's a thirty-foot monster, I'll head in the opposite direction. I'm downwind. If I'm careful not to be seen or heard, I can escape without being discovered. I'm pleased to find that I haven't lost all of my skills. I might be weak and burdened, but my skills as a hunter haven't abandoned me yet. I creep up to the bend in silence.

Two sharp cracks tell me the thing has just opened yet another small ribcage. The lungs will be removed. And then the heart crushed. For a moment, I wonder if the small creature might actually have survived up to this point.

Would I?

The horrible image nearly turns me around, but I'm too close to turn back. I slowly poke my head out around the bend—

—and instantly wish I hadn't.

5

The thing has its back to me, so I can't see its face, but the full head of red hair tells me this is a Nephilim. I expected as much—this place was designed to hold Nephilim—but the sight makes my insides twist with fear. It's crouched at the flat stone shore of a large lake. Or an ocean. I can't really tell because the orange liquid stretches to the horizon.

I duck away, breathing hard. There is nothing I fear more than the Nephilim. I have fought them. Killed them. But they broke me. Made me serve them. Respect them. Maybe even love them. And the remote possibility that I could be bent in that direction again horrifies me.

But could it happen here? In Tartarus?

I'm not sure, but if it did, I would regret it for all eternity.

In a flash, my course of action is reversed. I need to get away from this Nephilim. Bearing my burden on my own is hard enough. I take a step away from the lake and am stopped in my tracks by a high-pitched squeal. The dismantled creature is still alive, and shrieking in pain with its last breath.

A wet pop silences the creature.

Its heart has been crushed. I close my eyes. The poor thing.

A wail rips through the air. It's tortured, like the small creature's final scream, but louder and full of something else.

Anger.

Rage.

Confusion.

The tone and pitch of the voice fills me with a strange kind of understanding. The thing around the bend doesn't *want* to kill. It's compelled to. And it's tortured by that compulsion. This realization makes me reevaluate the situation. I gasp as a detail flies in the face of my assumptions.

The red hair coupled with the fact that this is Tartarus made me assume the killer is a Nephilim. But the height is all wrong. It—he—didn't look much bigger than me.

He's human, I think. *A hunter. But why would another hunter be here in Tartarus?*

Before I think too much about it, I slide back to the bend and take a peek. He's still there, crouched by the water, but he's not moving and his head is turned to the side slightly. Listening. To me.

He heard my gasp.

I'm sure of it.

There is no turning back now. No running. My only hope to avoid conflict is to make the first move a peaceful one.

I step out from hiding, doing my best to stand up straight and look tough. But my words are soft spoken and kind. "Are you all right?"

The question sounds ridiculous as it floats through the air. He sniffs with a single sharp intake of air. Is he smelling me? Or just surprised by my voice? Or my words?

"Do you need help?" I say.

The man's head spins toward me in a blur. Long tendrils of red hair whip around his face, concealing it from me. "Help!" he screams, sounding both offended and desperate. "Help!"

Then his hair falls away and I see his face.

My face.

"Ull?" The word flies from my mouth. Revulsion spreads through my body like thick, rotting syrup.

He's just as surprised as I am. "Solomon!" He falls backward and crab-crawls away from me until his hand slashes into the liquid lake. He screams in pain, lifting his now smoldering hand from the liquid. Not water.

Confusion sweeps across Ull's face, as I'm sure it does mine. This is a physical world. Ull has only ever existed in my mind. He's an aspect of my personality, not a living, breathing person. This makes no sense.

But he's still me. A part of me. And what he's doing is vile. "Why are you killing these creatures?" I ask.

He shakes his head quickly, eyes darting back and forth. He looks at everything but me. His breathing speeds up. He grinds his teeth.

"Ull!" I shout.

"Can't...stop!" he screams. The shaking grows worse, like he's about to explode. "Don't...want...this!"

"Ull," I say, feeling compassion for the violent me.

"Don't...want...to kill..." His eyes lock on me. "You." He's quick to his feet and I notice that unlike me, Ull is strong. Very strong. All sinewy with muscle and taut skin. His face is covered in stubble. While I retained all of my mental abilities, he retained our physical prowess. While we're both clearly dealing with emotions, Ull was never good at controlling his and the weight of this place must be crushing him—pushing him deeper into madness, to the point where he wants to kill me.

"You can't kill me," I say. "We're in Tartarus."

His eyes dart around again. He's trying to understand, but I suspect he's too far gone.

When he turns his head toward the sky and lets out a Nephilim howl, I know I'm right. He opens his hands, hooks his fingers into talons and charges. He's weaponless, dressed only in ragged leathers, but he's far quicker than I am. The best I can do as he closes the distance is raise my hands up.

Our hands collide first. Fingers entwine. A moment of resistance is followed by the tearing of flesh as his hands push down hard on the three blades of the climbing claws. He screams as the blades slip through flesh and bone before poking out from the back of his hands.

Then our bodies collide and I'm slammed into the stone wall behind me. My head collides with the wall and I hear a crack. I'm dazed, but conscious, and still pushing against Ull's arms with everything I've got. His strength has been sapped by the pain of the teeth piercing his hands, but he's still more than a match for me.

He roars at me, coating my face with spittle and blood. His mouth is bleeding. *He must have bitten his tongue when we collided*, I think. I feel pain in my mouth for a moment. *Why am I worried about him? He's trying to kill me!* "Get off me!" I scream.

"Die!" he shouts back. "Must die! Kill!"

I twist my hands, shifting the blades buried in his flesh.

He screams and then spews a few indiscernible lines.

My lips begin to quiver. Tears drip from my eyes. I've seen what he did to the small creatures. The pain he is about to inflict on me will be beyond comprehension. My arms weaken. "Please," I say. The word sounds more like a whimper. "Why are you doing this?"

"No!" he shouts. "No, no, no! Choice!"

No choice?

He doesn't want to kill me.

He didn't want to kill those creatures.

My arms lose the battle and slap back against the stone over my head. He's in my face now, his teeth chattering. He's going to bite me. I can see it in the way his head is turning. He's going to bite my nose off! But he's fighting it. Resisting.

"You can stop!" I shout back.

"C—can't!" His desperation matches my own. I'm shocked to see tears in his eyes, too. He doesn't want to hurt me. I am him. We are each other. And he's anything but self-destructive. "Need!"

His mouth opens, baring his teeth just inches from my nose. "Need!" he screams again.

I'm too terrified to speak now. The true pain of Tartarus is about to begin.

"Need...help!"

Help.

The word flashes into my mind.

Help.

I beheld in my dream, that a man came to him, whose name was Help.

I'm not the burdened traveler, I realize. *I...am Help. Ull is in the Slough. But how can I help him?*

Christian sank in the Slough of Despond because it amplified the burden he carried. The weight of the darkness of his heart overpowered him. I think about the awful things I've done. Most...were Ull. The weight on his shoulders must dwarf mine.

Escape from the Slough only came with Help's aid. *Give me thine hand: so he gave him his hand, and he drew him out.*

I look at our hands, bound by bone and blood.

The same blood.

The same burdens.

They do not belong to Ull alone. They are *ours* to bear.

I clench my fingers around Ull's hands, pulling him closer.

His head snaps back like he's been slapped in the face. "What are you doing?"

We look at our hands, no longer bound by fingers and bone, but by actual flesh. Our bodies are merging. The sight of it sends him into a panic. He draws away and manages to yank a hand free. But I hold on tightly and catch him around the base of his neck. He grinds his teeth, fighting to pull away, but I can feel his strength fueling my grip.

"What are you doing?" he screams.

"Helping," I say, pulling his head toward mine.

"Helping!?" His eyes dart up to our merged hands. There is only one hand now. Our hand. I understand his fear. I'm absorbing him. In a sense, I'm killing him the way he was just trying to kill me.

"Ull! Listen to me!" When his eyes meet mine, I instill my voice with the kind of affection my mother once used when I was hurt. "We can't fight each other anymore. Ninnis divided us. But we are not separate. We aren't Solomon *and* Ull. We are Solomon Ull Vincent."

The use of our last name takes the fight out of him some. "We need each other. We're weaker without each other."

He stiffens and is about to argue.

"We are incomplete," I say. "Intellect without emotion lacks power. Emotion without intellect lacks direction. We need to accept each other. We...need to be *I*."

His resistance fades, but I don't think this should be forced. We have been separated for a long time now and like submitting to the will of Nephil, I think this merger has to be a willing one. This needs to last.

"There are people depending on us," I say. "Em and Luca." There's a reaction, but it's not strong. Those relationships were formed when his personality was suppressed. "Mom and Dad," I say. He trembles with emotion. "And Aimee."

The memory of my birth fills my mind. Aimee holds me in her arms. Her smiling face is all I can see. I hear her voice, "You are a precious boy." They are some of the most powerful words ever spoken to me. I repeat them, speaking to Ull. "You are a precious boy."

We cry together, sharing our burdens, and in each other, we find uncommon strength. I feel Ull's forehead touch mine. His free hand wraps around my neck.

As one, we pull.

6

When I open my eyes, Ull is gone. It's just me, the gorge and the lake of burning fluid. I'm alone. *No*, I think, *Ull is here.*

I am Ull.

Solomon Ull Vincent.

I'm complete. Whole.

I look down and find my strong body returned. The stubble on my face tickles my hand as I rub it. The burden of my past failures still weighs upon me. But the burden is shared now. And bearable, despite being locked in Tartarus. In fact, in some ways I feel better than I have in a long time. There is no conflict in my thoughts. Only unity.

And apparently, that is against the rules.

The horn blast is deep and resonates through the land so powerfully that pebbles dance along the ground. The rumbling, monotone horn drones on for five seconds, shaking my body, and then stops. I can't be certain, but I suspect the horn is an alarm. That it sounds just moments after I've found a way to resist the power of this place is a little too coincidental for my taste.

The tower, I think. Whatever controls Tartarus must be there. This is a jail, after all. Someone must be in charge. Without any kind of debate or internal argument, the decision is made, and I set out at a run in the direction I last saw the tower. The ease with which I make up my mind brings a smile to my face. Split personalities are no fun.

The journey goes swiftly. The landscape is barren and inhospitable, but also easy to navigate. The footing is firm and free of any real obstacles. The only hindrances are the valleys, which twist and turn in unpredictable directions. After having to backtrack several miles, I've begun avoiding them altogether. At first, I stayed in the low lands as much as possible. After all, an alarm only sounds when there is a force that will respond to it. But I haven't seen another living thing in hours. Or days. Who knows? I no longer let the timelessness of Tartarus bother me.

I stop at the bottom of a stone hill. Its surface is covered with loose slabs of stone. I would normally skirt the edge of this rise, but it's tall and will provide me with an excellent view. The flat rocks slip under my feet and clatter loudly down the grade. Half way up, I start to question the wisdom of my ascent. I'm being far too noisy. But at this point, going down will make as much noise as finishing my climb. So I push onward.

Near the top, I crouch down low (as though I haven't already alerted anything nearby to my presence) and peer at the surrounding landscape. The endless stony expanse greets me anew. The orange sky is unchanged. I watch the turbulent clouds for a moment, wondering if it ever rains here, and if that rain is actually the acid-water held in the lake. That...would be horrible.

I see the tower clearly without the use of my telescope. I'm more than half way there. I trace the landscape back toward me, mapping the route I'll take, when my eyes land on a strange aberration. It's a cart. A wooden cart, like something a horse might pull, but oversized. It's empty except for what looks like patches of green mold and dark purple stains.

Dried blood.

Nephilim blood.

Before I can ponder my new discovery, I hear the gentle *tink, tink, tink,* of a stone bouncing down the hill behind me. Without a single thought, I leap over the top of the hill, dropping fifteen feet over the grade. I no longer have the ability to slow my descent with a gust of wind, but I have all of the knowledge and instincts of a hunter, and the skills to match. I land with a roll on the loose stone, which explodes away from my body and rattles down the hillside. As I come upright, I tug Whipsnap from my belt and stand my ground.

I watch the top of the hill, waiting. But nothing happens.

Perhaps the falling stone was a fluke caused by my presence on the hill. It's possible, but I definitely felt something behind me. And the cart stained with Nephilim blood... Someone brought it here.

"Show yourself!" I shout, and then smile. I can't help myself. My boldness and confidence feels right, but it's also new.

The ground shakes. Loose stones rattle and slide away. A plume of stone dust and debris billows from the top of the hill as a second impact resounds.

Why am I always picking fights with giants? And how did it sneak up behind me without making a sound?

The third impact brings a three-fingered hand over the top of the hill. The digits are at least three feet long, coated in mottled, gray skin and tipped with sharp, hooked fingernails.

Not a Nephilim. They have six fingers.

As the second hand comes over and I watch it pulverize the stone beneath its weight, I take a step back. Then the thing rises up over the crest, and I work hard to stifle my revulsion. The two gray hands are attached to long muscular arms. But each cluster of sinews is contained within skin. When the arm flexes, the separate strands of skinned muscles slap together. When relaxed they slide apart, and I can see through the spaces between them. The torso is built similarly, with each bunch of muscle wrapped in its own skin. Even more revolting is the thing's gut. What I assume are internal organs, hang from the stomach area, dangling by stretched out strands of skin. The pulsing, moving masses sway beneath it as the creature rises up over the hill.

But the absolute worst aspect of this thing is its head, or rather, heads. It has two of them. And like the rest of its body, the muscles controlling its face are separated and contained. It opens and closes its mouth, snapping its teeth together like it's tapping out Morse code. The enclosed cheek muscles hiss, as air slides through them. Its eyes are solid black, like a shark's—like a feeder's, but they lack the same malevolence, which surprises me. The thing is more indifferent. Like it doesn't care how things turn out. Or, perhaps more likely, like it already knows how things are going to turn out.

When it dips a head down to look at me, I see its skull and realize there is a third option. It's indifferent because it can't think for itself. Where there should be a rounded skull, there is a concave crater, like the back of its head was scooped away. The other head is the same. If there is any brain left in there, I'm not sure where it would be. But the creature is still functional. Still moving. And right now, I am the sole focus of its unflinching attention.

It has only revealed half of its mass and it's already over thirty feet tall. It's not quite Behemoth, but it dwarfs any Nephilim. I look down at Whipsnap's metal blade and spiked mace before turning my gaze back to the monster looming above me.

And then I do the only thing I can.

I run.

Loose shale slides down the hill, matching my speed. As I descend, I see that the wooden cart is far larger than I first thought. Easily big enough to pull a fully grown Nephilim warrior. Perhaps two. It occurs to me that the cart likely belongs to the creature behind me. And if that creature is moving bloodied Nephilim around, I don't stand a chance.

I pick up the pace and reach the bottom of the hill moments later. I veer left and head for what looks like another gorge. If I can reach a tight spot, I might slip away.

The sound of my quick breathing fills my ears. I focus beyond it and hear my bare feet slapping on the flat stone ground. Beyond that, I hear nothing.

No pounding footsteps.

No crush of stone.

No howl.

Nothing.

I risk a glance back. The thing is gone. The cart is still there, but the hilltop is barren. *What the—?*

A loud *boom* and a pressure wave strike me simultaneously. My forward momentum ceases and I'm thrown back. Dust rolls over me as I sit up. Holding my breath so I don't start coughing, I look up to find the monster standing before me. It's at least forty feet tall, but it's squatting on powerful hind legs, whose individually wrapped muscles ripple with energy. The sky above me is blotted out for a moment, like night has finally fallen, but the shades pull in and fold against the thing's back.

Wings! That's how it gets around so quietly.

Four large black eyes turn down toward me as the creature leans forward onto its hands. As it descends, its wrapped organs dangle close to the ground. One of them must be vital. If I can sever something important, maybe I can escape. I charge forward, beneath the giant. With all of my strength, I leap and instinctually will the wind to carry me forward. But the wind does not obey and I fall short, swinging out and striking the base of my target rather than the thin strand of flesh binding it to the creature's insides. I see the thin trace of a line where the blade met flesh, but there's no blood. I merely grazed the surface.

I'm struck in the side and sent sprawling. Whipsnap falls from my grasp. I'm still conscious, but when I sit up, a sharp pain and a near audible grinding in my side tell me several ribs are broken. *What hit me?*

For some reason, I am more disturbed by the thing's almost casual attack. It's not angry. Not growling or shrieking like the predators I'm used to. It's business as usual. So when it reaches down and plucks me from the ground, I lose my temper. I hurl insults and foul language that have been unused by my vocabulary, even when I was Ull the hunter.

My flung expletives are as useless as my weapons and skills.

The grip tightens, constricting my lungs.

I can't die, I tell myself. This is Tartarus. The afterlife. *I can't die. I can't die.*

The two massive heads watch me and then speak, each one saying a single word, forming complete sentences by speaking one at a time. "You *can* die in Tartarus," they say. "Again. Again. And again."

It's the first time I sense any kind of emotion from the thing. Pleasure.

It's going to enjoy what it's about to do.

The fist holding me turns to the ground and then stabs forward. With me in its grasp, the giant punches the stone ground. I shriek in pain. The impact breaks several of my bones and causes who knows how many internal injuries. Shock washes over me and the pain subsides some, but my mind begins to slip away.

I feel a breeze over my face as the fist draws up. My stomach lurches as it punches down again. The impact knocks the air from my lungs and my ribcage implodes. Consciousness fades quickly, but before I slip away, I feel my body rise and fall several more times. The monster is punching the ground, with me in its grasp.

Again.

Again.

And again.

7

I wake to the smell of blood. My keen nose, sharpened by my time as a hunter, recognizes the scent. It's *my* blood. But it's no longer fresh. Without opening my eyes, I reach out with my other senses. The first thing I notice is that I feel no pain. My body is healed. I can't smell anything beyond the strong scent of my blood. But I can tell that the blood is old. Dried.

How long have I been here?

I listen and at first hear nothing. But then there's something. Wind? I can hear the air moving, but cannot feel it on my skin. For a moment, I wonder if my immunity to the elements has returned, but then I feel the biting cold anew.

"You can open your eyes, little one."

The voice is deep and the words are spoken slowly. It's not the two-headed giant. The voice is different and comes from a single mouth. But I can tell the speaker is large, because despite being restrained, nearly a whisper, the voice still booms and echoes. I realize I'm in a large enclosed space, and then I open my eyes.

The ceiling above me is red and at least a hundred feet up. It reminds me of a cathedral, all arches, pillars and angles. But it lacks the decorum and opulence. This is simple, red stone. In fact, I think the space might have been carved from a single stone because there are no seams.

"You are impressed with Nyx?" The voice says.

You can hear my thoughts, I think at the thing.

"I prefer to speak."

"In English?" I say.

The Nephilim learned English from human teachers they kidnapped over the years. People like Aimee, who I kidnapped for them. But I seriously doubt there are human teachers here in Tartarus. Certainly not any that speak English, which in the grand scheme of humanity, is a relatively new language.

"I know all languages," says the voice. "You will have to face me eventually."

Mind readers can really be annoying sometimes. The conversation was bearable while staring at the ceiling. When I get a look at this thing, I suspect things might take a turn for the worse. But he's right. I'll have to face him eventually.

So I do. And what I see confuses me. He's a Nephilim. Maybe thirty feet tall, but he's seated on a slab of red stone jutting from the wall, so his height is hard to gauge. He has six fingers on each hand. I can't see his mouth, but I'd be willing to bet he has double rows of teeth, too. The problem I'm having is his hair. It's black. Not red.

The Nephilim, and the hunters, myself included, have blood red hair. It's an outward sign of their corruption. When a hunter leaves the Nephilim behind and seeks a life of goodness and peace, the color fades, to be replaced by the original hair color. And there is not a trace of red in this Nephilim's hair, not on his head, nor in his long beard.

He's dressed simply, in a white robe, and his six-toed feet are bare. Even more uncharacteristic, there is no metal band over his pulsing forehead. The Nephilim have many abilities granted to them by their unnatural parentage, including the ability to heal almost instantly. But their one weak spot is in the center of their forehead. It is an area usually protected by a golden band. But perhaps that weakness means nothing here in Tartarus, where things can die again, again, and again, as was so delicately proven to me by my two headed friend.

"You are confused?" the Nephilim says.

I get my feet under me. I'm typically afraid of Nephilim, but the fact that this one has black hair puts me at ease. I'm dressed in my normal clothes and Whipsnap lies on the floor beside me. I bend and pick up my weapon. The giant just watches as I wrap it around my waist and clip it to my belt.

The fact that this Nephilim hasn't shouted at me for not answering is also surprising. They are not known for their patience. I decide not to push it and say, "You're Nephilim?"

"You know I am," he replies.

"But, your hair?"

He gives a slow nod, acknowledging my confusion. "I am not corrupted."

"But your father…"

"A demon," he says. "Yes. I was one of the first born. An

accident. Overlooked by my father. Despite my…deformities, my mother kept me. And loved me. And raised me…as one of you."

A mother. A loving human mother with a Nephilim child. It sounds unbelievable, but if everything I've been taught about the twisted early days of mankind is the truth, then such a thing must have happened. And more than once.

"But my size soon made me stand out. As word spread, we learned that there were others like me. We were the first of our kind. Twelve of us. Titans among men. And soon, our fathers took notice."

Titans…

"Our fathers sought to corrupt us, to turn us against mankind, whom they detested. But we resisted them. Our human mothers, who had all passed away by that time, had taught us to care for, and protect mankind. But there was one… The eldest of us, the first born, who desired power more than anything else. He was seduced by our fathers, and quickly corrupted."

"Nephil," I say. The story is beginning to make sense.

"Nephil. Lord of the Nephilim, his followers. That is the name you know him by," the giant says. "I know him as Ophion."

I know the name. All of this is in my mind somewhere. I reach for the knowledge, seeking out the familiar words. Nyx. Ophion. Titans. Tartarus!

The information arrives in a flash. "You're a Titan," I say. "You were the Greek gods before being overthrown by Zeus and the Olympians, who are also Nephilim. When the Titans were defeated, they—you—were imprisoned in Tartarus!"

Before he can confirm or deny this information, I continue,

"Ophion. He was an evil Titan. The serpent. He ruled over the Earth long before the Olympians. But he was overthrown by Cronus, whose time on Earth is referred to as the Golden Age."

"Some of what you say is true. There was a war between the Titans and the younger generations of Ophion's followers now known as the Nephilim, but the Titans were not *confined* here. It is the Nephilim who *escaped*. Tartarus is a prison only for those whose hearts are dark. For the uncorrupted, it is an oasis. When the Titans realized that our time among men was causing more harm than good, we requested sanctuary. We were given Tartarus."

"Given by whom?" I ask.

"By the only one able to give such a thing." It is a horribly vague answer, but the story continues without elaboration. "When the Nephilim felt the weight of what they had become, and refused to change, Tartarus became unbearable. They fled. Fearing for mankind, the Titans fought to imprison the Nephilim, but most of them escaped."

"But not Ophion," I say.

"Ophion escaped Tartarus. But I gave chase and slew my brother before he could begin dominion over humanity."

"*You* defeated Ophion," I say. "You—you're Cronus!"

The giant actually grins and dips his head in a bow.

"It pleases me that my name is still known among men."

I don't tell him that very few people would actually recognize the name, let alone remember the history of it. He's generally not given more than a few sentences in history books or encyclopedias, often as a footnote to the more popular Greek gods.

"And what about the giant with two heads?" I ask

"Eurymedon, king of the Gigantes," he says. "My friend. The Gigantes, like the Titans and the Nephilim, have unnatural parentage. But they are not conceived; they are created—designed—from our blood. You would call them experiments."

"Like science?" I ask, a little surprised.

"Science is the word humanity uses for the supernatural once it understands the processes involved. Some would call the creation of the Gigantes science. Others would call it magic. It's just a matter of perspective."

"That's why he looks different?"

The nod is nearly imperceptible.

"How many Gigantes are here?"

"An army," he says. I want to ask more, but Cronus continues his story. "With Ophion's spirit freed from his body, he returned to Tartarus, occasionally causing unrest among the other Nephilim still confined to Tartarus."

"Do they ever try to leave?" I ask.

"From the inside, the gates no longer open to the unworthy," he says.

"But from the outside," I add, "anyone can open the gates."

He nods. "The Nephilim outside Tartarus fear this place. To return would mean staying for eternity. But *someone* did open the gates." The emphasis he puts on the word "someone" is angry, and directed toward me. "And Ophion left." The giant shakes his head, confused by the notion. "Ophion returned to the world as a spirit, which cannot last for our kind. I did not wish this fate on my brother, but it was the fate he chose."

My limbs suddenly feel heavy and I nearly vomit.

He doesn't know.

"What don't I know?" His voice is loud now. Barely contained anger. He might not be Nephilim, but that doesn't mean he won't get angry, and as the two-headed giant proved, violence isn't exactly forbidden here.

Before I can answer, I feel him enter my mind. Before he was simply listening to my conscious thoughts. Now he's digging through my memories. And he doesn't have to dig far. The events that led me here are still fresh in my mind. I feel myself transported back. I'm standing before the gates of Tartarus, facing the black spirit of Nephil as he enters my body.

I fall to my knees, screaming, reliving the most horrible experience of my life. And as I feel Nephil's darkness take control of my body and reach out for the world, the weight of Tartarus constricts me with pain beyond description. But the experience is different this time. I'm not just seeing things from my perspective. I'm in Nephil's head, too. And in that moment, I feel exactly what he did when his power merged with my own. The Earth's crust rotated, quickly, causing tidal waves, volcanoes, flash freezing. Catastrophe on a global scale. Billions. Billions dead. And it was just the beginning of Ophion's vengeance. The memory concludes with my rejection of Nephil and his subsequent bonding with Ninnis.

I fall back on the floor as though flung by a powerful force. My body convulses several times and I dry-heave. I wish I could erase the memory, now complete with Nephil's perspective, from my mind. I clutch my eyes shut, willing it away, but it's not until

I hear, and feel, Cronus's heavy feet pounding toward me that I can think of anything else. When I open my eyes to see Cronus above me, what I see is nearly as bad. A long segmented tail, like a scorpion's, slides out from behind the giant. It is tipped with a curved, blade-like stinger that looks like a sickle.

Cronus's sickle.

The tail rises above me, poised to strike.

8

The strike comes so fast and sudden that my eyes don't even register the movement. One second the tail is wavering above me with menacing intent. The next, it's stopped, just inches from my face. A bead of liquid forms at the tip of Cronus's sickle-like tail. *It's a stinger*, I realize. And I have no doubt the effects of being stung will make me wish I could die.

"Wait!" I shout. "We're on the same side!"

Cronus stomps his foot. The impact shakes the floor beneath me. "You gave yourself to him!"

"And I rejected him!" Cronus saw this in the memory, but he might have been so distracted by the rest that he failed to register why Nephil left my body.

"You set him free!"

This, unfortunately, is the truth. Without me present, Nephil would have remained bound to Tartarus forever. "I had no choice!"

The tail pulls back a few feet so Cronus can look at me. His yellow eyes burn into me, searching for deception. "There is always a choice."

"You understand what it means to surrender something important to save the ones you love," I say. "You did the same thing for humanity. You left and came to Tartarus, but the Nephilim escaped. You tried to do the right thing, but there was a negative consequence."

Cronus says nothing. He's listening.

"I did the same thing," I say. "Nephil needed me to leave Tartarus. It's true. And I willingly offered myself to him. That is also true."

Cronus tenses, so I speak fast. "But I never intended to let him survive. I thought he would cease to exist once I forced him out. I didn't know he would find another vessel. I didn't realize how strong Ninnis was. You have to believe me. Search my memories again. Go back further."

And he does.

Since I'm a willing participant this time, the experience is far less disturbing. We watch my life in reverse: my recent merging with Ull, the battle with Nephil outside the gates of Tartarus, Luca—the reason for me being there. Cronus pauses.

"You were there for the boy?"

"Yes."

"He is innocent."

"He is."

"He is…you."

I don't answer. Cronus finds it in my memories of Luca. He understands. But then he goes back further. To my time as a hunter. The awful things I did. My training under Ninnis. My breaking. My kidnapping.

Further now. The trip to Antarctica. Mira. Aimee. Merrill. My parents, my birthday and Justin. My childhood. He slows the rewind around age six. My hair is cut in a ridiculous bowl cut, but I'm otherwise identical to Luca. The rest of my life in reverse plays back in a flash, ending with Aimee's smiling face. He lingers here, sensing the significance of this moment. But it's not Aimee's smile or the love radiating from her that has caught his attention.

It's something else.

Something I never noticed before.

The memory starts over at the beginning. The very beginning.

I am warm. And then…cold. The darkness breaks and blurry light stabs my eyes. I've never seen light before. The pain makes me squirm. But I can't cry out. My lungs are filled with fluid. But I'm not in danger. I can feel the life giving pulse at my stomach. I didn't know what it was back then, only that it gave me life, but now I realize it was my umbilical cord. The pulse slows, and then, it's gone, separated from my body. I try to scream now, but the liquid in my lungs is still there and everything feels wrong.

My tiny mouth is pushed open and something enters my throat. The pressure in my chest disappears. Instinctually, I take a breath.

And that's when it happens. A wave of energy ripples through my newborn body.

The cold disappears.

My senses clear.

As does my vision.

I can feel the world outside. As though it's a part of me.

Somewhere, far away, an ice shelf the size of Los Angeles breaks free from the continent. The snap is powerful and violent. I start screaming, unable to comprehend first being separated from my mother, and then being connected to something so much larger. The memory ends as Aimee draws me up to her face and smiles.

I snap out of the past and back into the present. Cronus stumbles back and plops back onto his chair. He's lost. And to be honest, so am I. I'd never gone that far back. My memories begin with Aimee's face. But in the few seconds before that, when I drew my first breath, I bonded with the continent, and I could feel it. It strengthened me. Made me immune to the cold. And it frightened me. The shock of it must have blocked that memory.

"I…do not understand," Cronus says. The way he has his head in his hands is so very human that it shocks me. "You have been given a most unusual gift, the likes of which have not been bestowed on a human being in thousands of years. After the great flood, in which many Nephilim perished, the Nephilim were still above ground and active among humans. I stayed in contact with humanity, teaching leaders how to resist the Nephilim corruption, how to defend against attack and even how a boy with a stone could slay the mighty Nephilim. On occasion, heroes would rise up, blessed with abilities and weapons beyond understanding. And over time, the Nephilim were pushed back to the land where all things began. As the land froze, they fled underground, nearer to the gate than they preferred and bound by ice and snow. It is then that my contact with humanity came to a close and I believed the days of heroes had come to an end."

He opens his arms toward me. "Yet here you are. A human. In Tartarus. Whose life was touched by light at birth, destined to rise up, a hero, against not just the Nephilim, but my old nemesis, Ophion, as well."

I'm confused and more than a little intimidated by the things he's suggesting, which includes me being chosen, at the moment of my birth, to do battle with the Nephilim. Did I ever have a chance at a normal life? Or did some higher power move me like a chess piece?

"You are not a pawn," Cronus says, reading my thoughts.

"Get out of my head!" I shout.

"Your thoughts are strong," he says. "I can no more shut out your shouted thoughts than I can erase the moon by closing my eyes."

"You can see the moon? Here?" I ask, suddenly confused.

He shakes his head, no. "I do miss it sometimes."

"We went there," I say. "To the moon. People did."

He grins, confirming my belief that he had two rows of teeth. "I have always marveled at the ingenuity of humanity. Your individual lives are short. Just a blink. But collectively, from time's start to its completion, humanity is capable of amazing things."

"Like defeating Nephilim."

"On occasion."

"You said I was touched by light at birth," I say, but never get to form my question, as he seems to know it already.

"You believe, as do the Nephilim, that the strength and abilities granted you at your birth came from the corruption of the Nephilim spirit possessing the continent you call Antarctica."

"Antarktos," I whisper, remembering the word Dr. Merrill Clark preferred to use for the continent. Cronus looks at me oddly. I'm not sure if it's because I've interrupted him or because of the word I spoke.

"Antarktos," he says. "I prefer it as well. The Nephilim have many rituals; some are affective and give them access to the supernatural world, and our fathers. Others, like the spilling of their blood into the bowels of Antarktos, are futile efforts to claim the land as their own. There is no spirit of the Nephilim possessing the land. And it certainly did not fill you at the moment of your birth. If it had, you would embrace them, not resist them."

"But what about the dark thoughts?" I ask. When I was younger, my imagination would sometimes veer in horrible directions. If I stood near a knife, I would imagine picking it up and stabbing it into the chest of whoever stood nearby. The thoughts came fast and always left me disturbed. "You saw them, didn't you?"

Cronus cracks his knuckles. It sounds like his big bones are actually snapping, but he shows no discomfort. "Humanity contains the potential for both good and evil. As do Titans and Nephilim, though we are more inclined toward the negative thanks to our fathers' influence. It is the choice you make that defines you, not the conjuring of your imagination. You abhor the dark thoughts, as you do Nephil. The darkness has always sought you out, perhaps more than others, but you have repelled it. That it exists doesn't make it part of you."

"Then I'm not the only one?" I ask.

"Listening to the darkness or not is a decision every human being must make every day of their lives. Most, like you, resist. But some accept the darkness. Some become slaves to it. To the Nephilim. And while you might see acts of violence in your mind's eye, even the darkest heart sometimes sees beauty, or imagines an embrace or love."

"Why are you telling me this?" I ask. "It doesn't make any sense. You say that I was given a gift that makes me uniquely suited to defeat the Nephilim, yet I'm here, in Tartarus, forever. What good am I? You saw what happened. Nephil took control. He used that power—my power—and nearly wiped out the planet. Billions died. Billions!"

Cronus's head turns to the floor.

"This war with the Nephilim has brought humanity to the brink once before."

I'm about to argue when I remember something he said earlier. "The flood." I don't question that it happened. A global flood is recorded in nearly all of the planet's myths, histories and religious texts. What doesn't make sense is what good a flood would be against the Nephilim. Unless... "Nephilim can drown?"

He nods.

"That's great," I say. "But it doesn't change the fact that I caused the deaths of billions."

"Nephil did that," he says, growing impatient. "Not you. You will never defeat him if you are already beaten in your mind."

"Don't you understand?" I shout. "I can't beat him. I'm stuck here. With you. Forever."

"Have you considered that, to defeat Nephil, you first had to enter Tartarus?"

I meet his eyes. What's he getting at? "I'm stuck here."

"Maybe you needed to speak to me first?"

He's ignoring me. Great.

"Maybe you needed to come here, to a place where your two halves could be reconciled?"

That's a pretty good point actually, but it still doesn't change the fact that I'm stuck. In Tartarus. With no way out.

"Or maybe you needed to learn about a weapon that can shake the very foundations of any Nephilim citadel?"

This catches me off guard. "A weapon?"

"And maybe, if you stopped to *think* about something other than your own personal struggles for just a moment, you would realize that you are, in fact, no more a prisoner here, than I."

I just stare at him.

Cronus grins. Despite his sharp rows of teeth, it lacks none of the malevolence seen in Nephilim smiles. "For the worthy, all that separates this world from the other is a door. And you, Solomon, were deemed worthy at birth. All you need do, is push."

9

The gates of Tartarus are a half mile off, but stand high above me. Cronus carried me here on his shoulders, saying nothing as he walked. He didn't say anything more about Tartarus, the Gigantes or this supposed weapon. He simply walked. I'm not sure if it's the aberration of time, or Cronus's long legs, but we seem to cover the distance quickly.

Cronus stops at the top of a rise. He looks around, takes a deep breath and lets it out, the way I used to after rain on a warm spring day. Despite Cronus ignoring all of my questions since the journey began, I ask, "What are you smelling? The air is dry and cold."

He turns his head toward me. His mouth, which could bite me in two, is just a few feet away. "You still carry your burden."

"What?"

"I can sense its weight. It blinds you."

I remember what he said earlier. Tartarus is only a place of torture for those unwilling to change. Unwilling to give up their burden. Like the Slough of Despond. It's the weight that pulls you under, not the swamp. "But I did those things. I'm responsible. Even more so, now that I'm fully Ull and fully Solomon. I can't attribute the awful things I did to another personality."

"Claiming responsibility is not the same as accepting forgiveness. Or redemption. Everyone makes mistakes, Solomon. Everyone must be forgiven at one time or another. Some lie. Some murder."

I slip in, "Some destroy the planet."

"*That* was not you." He picks me up off his shoulder and places me on the ground. "I have seen your ability to forgive, little one. I saw what you did for Ninnis. And for Kainda. But your ability to forgive is worthless if you cannot turn it upon yourself. If you do not, the darkness you seek to defeat will eat you from the inside."

"Someone has to offer me forgiveness for those things," I argue. "How am I supposed to ask the billions—" He raises an eyebrow. "Right. That wasn't me. Still, how can I earn something like forgiveness?"

Cronus crouches down, but his eyes are still far above me. "Forgiveness cannot be earned. It can only be granted and received. I sense you need to hear the words." He puts an arm-sized finger under my chin and lifts my head to face him. "Solomon, for your crimes against your fellow men, for the darkness of your heart and for the evil thoughts of your mind, you are forgiven."

My lips squeeze tight. *It can't be that simple!*

"It is that simple," he says. "You need only accept."

A strange emotion wells up inside me. I fight it, but cling to it at the same time. The weight lifts. I fall to my knees as pinpricks of pain ripple over my skin. Apparently, in Tartarus you can literally feel the burden being yanked away. And then, it's gone. I gasp a breath and find the air sweeter. Refreshing.

Full of thanks and relief, I step forward and wrap my arms around Cronus's leg. If Em could see me now. Solomon, the great Nephilim slayer, hugging a Titan.

Cronus rubs my head with the tip of his finger. "Solomon," he whispers. "Look again."

I loosen my grip and step back. After wiping the wetness from my eyes, I look. The hills are no longer barren. Thick green grass, full of flowers, covers the land. The sky has turned blue. The distant lake is shimmering and peaceful, and I have no doubt I could swim its water without fear of melting. But the most startling aspect of the transformed scenery is the tower. It's no longer made of hard stone. It's a tree. A massive tree stretching high into the sky. Above the tree is a light source, as bright as the sun, but indistinct.

"What…"

"The secrets of Tartarus are too many to tell," he says before I can ask. "You have been here long enough."

"How long?" I ask.

"Three months," he says.

Three months. It sounds like a long time, but it could have been a hundred years and not felt any different to me. I'm about to ask him if three months Tartarus time is the same as three months surface time, but don't. I think he knows exactly what I meant when I asked. "You mentioned a weapon."

"The Jericho Shofar."

My face screws up involuntarily. He can't be serious. "A shofar? A ram's...horn?"

"Like you," he says, "The Jericho Shofar is...unique. Touched by the light. And in the right hands, a powerful weapon. One you will need."

"What does it do?" I ask.

To my surprise, Cronus shrugs.

I can't help but laugh. This is ridiculous. "You don't even know what it does!"

"It was used by a man named Joshua to—"

"Destroy the walls of Jericho," I say. "It's a story from the Old Testament. Joshua destroyed the city and killed everyone inside."

"Every*thing* inside," he says. "Jericho, as you know from your time underground, was a Nephilim city. The horn was used to defeat them."

"New Jericho," I say. He's right.

"Where can I find the horn?" I ask.

Again, he shrugs. "I only know who to ask about it."

"Who?"

He grins, this time I sense mischief. "Hades."

I throw up my hands. "Hades! C'mon. Not only is he Nephilim, but he's also the god of the underworld. Of hell!"

Cronus shakes his head. "That humanity has survived so long is a miracle. Has your mythology skewed everything? You have lived in the underworld for years, at times quite comfortably. Would you call it hell?"

"Antarktos is the underworld?" I ask. He doesn't need to

answer the question. It's clearly what he meant. It's just surprising.

"Hades is one of my oldest friends. The underworld—the land beneath Antarktos—was his domain long before the Nephilim sought refuge there. He was here, in Tartarus, for a time, and he felt his burden lifted. But when the Nephilim left, he went with them."

"You couldn't stop him?" I ask.

"I...sent him."

"You *what*?"

"I needed someone to watch them, to observe, and to report back on occasion."

"A spy?"

He waggles a finger in the air. "But...be careful when you approach him. I have not heard from him in some time and fear he may have finally been corrupted."

"How long is a long time?" I ask.

He says nothing.

It feels strange, bullying an answer out of a Titan, but I need to know. "*How...long?*"

"Nearly one thousand years."

Great. "So I find Hades, tell him Cronus says hello, see if he eats me and then say, 'By the way, do you know where I can find the Jericho Horn?'"

The giant chews on his lips for a moment and then nods. "Precisely."

"That's got to be one of the worst plans I've ever heard," I say.

"But..."

Jerk. The mind-reading giant already knows the punch line. He just wants to hear me say it. *Fine.* "It's better than most of mine."

"I thought you would like it." He raises his hand up toward the massively tall black doors built into a cliff side that rises up into the clouds. "It's time for you to go."

"What do I do with the horn once I have it?" I ask. "Am I supposed to kill the Nephilim? Bring them here?"

"I do not know," he says. "I wish I did. Your destiny might be known only to others, but it has always been in your hands." He shoos me away, nudging me with his big hand and then waving me forward. "Go."

I move toward the gates, but walk backward so I can see him. There's a lot I want to ask, and say. I have never been friends with a creature like Cronus. There's so much I could learn from him. And this place, this paradise…how could anyone want to leave here? How could Hades stay away?

As this thought absorbs my attention, I trip and spill backwards. I manage to turn the fall into a graceful roll, but it's still embarrassing. I'm supposed to defeat Nephil, aka Ophion, and an army of Nephilim and hunters, and I can't even walk backwards. When I look up, Cronus is smiling and shaking his head.

I grin back at him, wave, turn to the gates and run. The grass is soft beneath my feet. The speed and the warm breeze washing over my face invigorate me. I cover the distance in a flash and find myself standing before a wall of black.

The gates of Tartarus.

All you need do, is push.

I place my hand against the cold black metal. It doesn't seem possible that anything could open this massive door, human, Nephilim or Gigantes.

It opens for the worthy, and you were deemed worthy at birth.

I'm not sure I agree, but I decide to believe the Titan.

So, I push.

10

The massive door slips open silently, as though oiled by whatever WD-40 equivalent is available in Tartarus. The blackness of the door is replaced by a veil of more blackness. Even open, one cannot see the real world from Tartarus, or vice versa. But, according to Cronus, I can step through.

I take a look back, hoping for an encouraging nod, but Cronus is gone. I'm tempted to stay for a moment, as I look out at the paradise that revealed itself after my burden was lifted. *How could the Nephilim not want to be here?* I wonder. Then again, they're all about hate, killing and pain. Of course, it's far more baffling that even the Nephilim could find forgiveness here, if they wanted to. It doesn't seem right, that such a deep-rooted evil could ever have the opportunity for redemption.

Then I remember Ninnis, whose heart is as dark as any Nephilim. Worse, if you consider that he is fully human. The Nephilim are half demon. They were born at a moral disadvantage. But then there is Cronus and the other Titans.

Evil is a choice, I decide. Human or demon, there is a choice.

There is always a choice. Cronus's words.

But what about the hunters? Broken so that their former self is gone. They're turned into killers. Like I was.

But there is still a choice. Tobias, Em, Xin and maybe even Kainda chose to fight the will of their masters. There is always a choice.

There is always hope.

Step through, I tell myself. *Stop delaying.*

I raise my hand and place it through the veil. It tingles, but I feel nothing else. There could be an army waiting for me. Or Behemoth. Or Ninnis.

No, I think. *No one is waiting.* As far as they know, Tartarus is a one-way trip. Not to mention it's been three months since I left. At most, there will be a hunter on watch. And that, I can handle.

I step through, eyes open.

The world turns black and then resolves again, like walking through a shadow. My eyes quickly adjust to the low light of the massive cavern on the other side, and I flinch back, nearly falling back into Tartarus.

Behemoth is waiting for me.

But there's something wrong with the creature.

The massive body is shorter. Is it squatting? It's leaned against the cavern wall, just to the right of the gates. Its mouth hangs open, revealing rows of giant triangular teeth. The body is limp. The long, red, tentacle-like hair hangs in loose bundles.

Is it sleeping? I wonder.

Then my senses pick up more details. The body lacks mass, as though deflated. The skin hangs loose in places. The normally black eyes are milky white and shriveled. And then there is the stench of decay.

Behemoth is dead.

I don't even think Nephil could kill the giant beast on his own.

With my eyes turned toward the towering corpse, I step forward and I'm once again given cause to jump back. I've stepped in a puddle of water.

Cold water.

My powers have not yet returned.

As the chill of the underworld wraps itself around me, I realize how easy I've had it all this time. The other hunters live in the underworld, never complaining about the constant fifty-five degree temperature, while I've been living in temperature-free bliss. If my powers don't return soon, I'm going to have to have to adapt to the cold.

But there is something else confusing about this puddle—the fact that it exists at all. When I last stood in this spot, moments before stepping back into Tartarus, no water flowed through this portion of Behemoth's cavern. I look up and find the cavern floor littered with puddles. Even the air is moist.

My eyes return to Behemoth's dead body, the mouth upturned and agape, as though gasping for air.

He drowned, I think. *Behemoth drowned. The whole cavern must have flooded. But how is that possible?*

A gentle scratching sound pulls my attention down to the

massive, shriveled stub of flesh that used to be Behemoth's leg. I step closer, watching as a small spot of flesh the size of my fist pulses in and out, as though being poked from within. When I'm ten feet away, the skin tears and one of the underworld's most common denizens—the giant albino centipede—slips out. This one is bigger than most. In fact, it might be the biggest specimen I've ever seen. The portion emerging is three feet long and nearly as thick as a football. If the proportions of this centipede match the ones I'm used to, it's at least another six feet long!

Big enough to put up a fight.

Big enough to eat me.

When it senses my presence, it stops and turns its head toward me. Its two antennae dance in the air. This is the point where the creatures usually identify me as a hunter and attempt to flee.

This one stands its ground.

Oookay.

I feel like I've stepped into a world as foreign as Tartarus. Nothing here matches what I remember or what I expect.

A sharp clatter vibrates from the centipede as its mandibles twitch. This is new to me, too. What is it doing?

My answer comes from Behemoth's body. At first, it's just a few spots of raised flesh, then a hundred. Then a thousand. One by one, centipedes emerge from Behemoth's mass. So many tear out of the stomach area that the flesh falls away in a giant sheet, revealing a squirming mass of living insides.

Centipedes. Some reaching twenty feet in length. They've been eating Behemoth from the inside out, and from the looks of it, have finished off pretty much everything worth eating. Not only are they big. Not only do they number in the thousands.

But they're also hungry.

The staple food of the underground has become an apex predator. And based on the chatter emerging from the swarm, they're also communicating. Coordinating.

I'm so dead.

For a moment, I think about retreating, back into Tartarus. But then I'd really be trapped there. No, I can't go back. I need to push forward.

I need to get the hell out of here.

So I run.

And after my first few steps, I realize I might not be a fast enough runner. The mass of centipedes falls toward me like a living avalanche. If they catch me, they'll tear me to pieces and devour me in a matter of seconds. My legs begin to cramp, as I will them to move faster. If my abilities had returned, I could fling myself out of reach with a gust of wind, but every time I reach out for that connection to the continent, I slow. So I ignore what I could have done in the past and focus on what is possible now.

The sound of thousands of sharp legs taps on the stone floor to my right. I glance over and see the outer edge of the living wave about to collide into my side. I dive forward, just out of reach and roll back to my feet. A smaller centipede specimen is flung from the mass and collides with my back. I nearly fall over, but manage to stay on my feet. I keep moving, even as the three-foot long creature stabs its mandibles into my forearm. I try to shake it off, but its segmented body coils around my arm and constricts.

It's not trying to kill me, I realize. *It's trying to slow me down.*

"Fine," I say to the centipede, "you're coming with me."

As I veer off to the left, heading for one of the side tunnels, I realize it's a mistake. The tunnels surrounding the cavern are either tight squeezes or riddled with obstacles that will slow me down. Every single one of them leads uphill. And most connect with a maze of other tunnels through which the centipedes could speed ahead and lay in wait. The point is, I can't outrun them in the side tunnels. So I push forward, hoping they'll tire, but I doubt that's going to happen.

I glance back.

A mistake.

The writhing wave of centipedes is just ten feet back. The one attached to my arm senses the end approaching and squeezes harder. I shout in pain, but then hear a roar over my own voice. It's deep and constant—not from a living thing.

As the moisture in the air grows so thick that it starts collecting on my skin, I know what lies ahead.

A river.

And the centipedes can't swim.

As I round a bend in the giant cavern, the river comes into view. It emerges from one side of the cave, races across the nearly two-mile distance and exits out the other end. It's thirty feet across and filled with raging white rapids. I don't stop to think when I reach the water's edge. I simply jump.

As my feet leave the ground and the wet wind above the river strikes my side, I will it to carry me across to safety. I feel the wind kick up around me…

And then I drop like a stone into the wash of white.

The water is freezing cold. The centipede on my arm reacts immediately, trying to unwrap itself from my arm. But I hold on tight. I'm going to need it if I escape the river.

As I'm swept away, I look back and see that a few of the centipedes have fallen into the water. They writhe and then slip beneath the waves. Drowned and dead. The rest pile up along the shore, heads tracking me as I'm carried away. Behemoth might be dead, but Tartarus has a new guardian.

I lose sight of them as I'm pulled into the cavern's sidewall and plunged into darkness.

11

After being pummeled by miles of racing rapids that twist through the underworld, I manage to scramble out of the widening waters and pull myself up onto a slab of gray stone. The centipede on my arm has long since drowned, but it's still attached in a death grip. As my energy wanes, I unravel the creature from my arm and tug each mandible out of my flesh. I barely feel it thanks to the numbing cold of the river, but my blood flows freely. As I sense unconsciousness looming, I unhitch Whipsnap from my belt and use the mace end to bludgeon the centipede's head. There's no way to know if the centipede's physiology was affected by consuming Behemoth and I don't want to risk it reviving while I sleep.

I glance down at the twin wounds in my forearm. The blood is dripping onto the stone and running into the river. I should really take care of it. The scent of blood will draw predators to me. But my exhausted body gives me no choice. I lie down as my vision fades and place my head on stone ground.

"Have a cookie," Aimee says to me. She's standing in her room at Asgard, but there is a modern oven. She pulls out a tray of steaming cookies and holds it out to me. The cookies are centipede heads. "They're just as sweet as brown sugar. Just don't tell anyone I gave one to you or they'll slit my throat." The words are spoken with a broad white grin, as though everything is just dandy.

"Can I have one?" asks a small voice that I recognize.

I look at myself sitting in the corner. I'm six years old. And hungry. So hungry. I watch myself pick up a centipede head cookie and eat it with gusto. The cookie disappears in three bites and then the boy-me licks his fingers. "Thank you, Mrs. Clark." Then, strangely, he notices me. How can I notice myself in a dream?

I look confused. Then, with a flash of wide-eyed excitement, the boy-me says, "Solomon? Is it really you?"

Now I'm confused. I'm talking to myself?

"Solomon, don't you recognize me?" the boy says. "It's Luca."

"Luca!" I sit bolt upright, wide awake. I'm in the cave by the river.

Was it really Luca? In the past, the six-year-old version of me has seen events through my eyes. Usually moments of high emotion. But that bond has been broken for three months while I was in Tartarus. Perhaps being chased by the centipedes retriggered that connection, but it was delayed so that it occurred during my dream, instead of during the actual high stress event? That's my best guess, anyway.

Pain pulses up my arm and begs for my attention. The wound is caked in dry blood, as is much of the stone upon which I lay. *Strange*, I think, *a predator should have found me.* I was an easy meal, and easy meals in the underground are essentially unheard of. Not that I'm complaining. Not being eaten in my sleep is a good thing. I just don't understand it.

Several needs strike me all at once. In the three months I spent in Tartarus, I neither ate nor drank. Sustenance was not required there. I slide down to the water's edge, dip my good arm into the frigid water and cup several mouthfuls to my lips. While I'd like to dunk my head in the water and drink until my belly distends, I remember my hunter discipline and ration it out, careful not to shock my dehydrated system. After drinking, I wash the dry blood from my arm. The river sweeps the red powder downstream. A predator is eventually going to come calling.

Momentarily sated, I slide back up the bank and turn my attention to the centipede. The small knife I carry is quite sharp. It's the perfect tool for separating the sinewy flesh that holds the centipede's shell together. I carve along both sides, and then reach under the base of the carapace, which was severed from the head when I crushed it. With a quick yank, three feet of segmented centipede carapace peels away, revealing a row of segmented dollops of rank, white flesh. At first glance, the meat looks solid, like lobster, but when removed from the body, it turns to something like pasty oatmeal slathered in lard.

I scoop some of the flesh paste onto my fingers and rub it over the wounds inflicted by the centipede. It's disgusting, but the flesh expedites healing and fights infection. With the wounds covered, I flick the paste off my hand and wrap my arm with cloth bandages I've used in the past.

My wounds have been tended to. My thirst has been quenched. All that's left is my hunger. I scoop out a larger wad of centi-flesh and slop it into my mouth. I wince at the flavor. The normally offensive food is bad enough when eaten regularly, but after three months without food, it's downright vile. After swallowing the mouthful, I nearly throw up, but manage to keep it, and three more bites down. As I eat, I remember the last time I had this meal, with Em, just before facing Ninnis and Nephil at the gates of Tartarus. Centipede is far more bearable when shared with a friend. At least then, you can laugh at each other's disgusted expressions.

Thinking of Em gets me to my feet. I stretch and twist my body in preparation for traveling in the underground. I'm still cold, but it pales in comparison to the chill experienced in Tartarus. *I can manage it*, I tell myself, and I can always build a fire. Dung is the fire fuel of the underworld, and it's usually not hard to find. Feeling slightly more prepared for the journey ahead, I look to the stone wall, find a fissure and slip inside.

Moving through the underworld puts me at ease. It's like returning home after a long vacation. Its familiarity is welcome. Now if only I had a destination.

I need to go up. To the surface. It's where Em and Luca will be hiding. But Antarktos is the size of the United States. Finding someone on the surface could take a lifetime. Maybe longer.

Especially if they're hiding and skilled at it. Even if I did know where they were, I don't know where I am. I've never been in this part of the subterranean world. But I've got a good sense of direction, even without the sun to guide me. And sooner or later, I'm bound to come across a tunnel I recognize.

But everything seems different. Not only are these tunnels unfamiliar, but the scents of the underworld are off. Actually, they're gone. I should be able to smell traces of animal feces, urine, fungi and blood almost everywhere. Fresh blood stands out from the rest, but there is always an underlying stench of life in the underworld. But there is none of that now. It's like the whole place has been scrubbed clean.

Could the flood that killed Behemoth have affected the entire underworld? Could everything be dead?

No. I'd smell the decay.

Unless everything were swept away.

But to where? There would be pockets of trapped flesh everywhere. The underworld would reek of death, even three months later. No, this is different. I think everything, and everyone, has left. All the flood did was clean away the filth.

But not all of it. A strange odor reaches my nose. It's like a mix between Nephilim blood and something antiseptic. Or chemical. It's a smell that makes no sense in the underworld. Curious, I follow the scent path and exit into a large, unnatural tunnel leading up at a steep angle. The walls are smooth and barren of decoration except for two lines of glowing yellow stones spaced four feet apart. A large staircase twisting up through the tunnel sports four-foot tall steps—sized for a Nephilim warrior. A second staircase, with steps sized for human beings, runs parallel.

The tunnel is curved, so I can't see what lies in either direction, but I sense up is the way to go, and I begin my ascent. Despite the odd smell, I haven't detected any trace of something living. The Nephilim blood is disconcerting, but it smells old. Dry and powerless. Still, I keep a hand on Whipsnap, just in case.

The smooth stairs, so unlike the rest of the world, feel strange beneath my feet. In fact, everything about this tunnel is odd. I run my hand along the wall as I follow the steps up. The surface feels polished. Like velvet. It speaks of a precision I didn't believe the Nephilim capable of. They're more brutish. And violent. More likely to create a tunnel by smashing the stone with their bare hands than something so...clean.

The feeling of cleanliness increases. The tunnel feels *more* than clean.

It feels sterile.

I reach the top of the stairs and quickly understand why. Though to say I understand what I'm looking at isn't accurate, because it makes no sense.

12

The space is more like a modern room than a cavern, in that it, like the tunnel, was carved from the stone with precision. It's a giant rectangle, fifty feet tall, maybe two hundred wide and three times as long. The ninety degree angles where the walls meet each other, the floor, and the ceiling are all perfect, and seamless, hewn right out of the solid stone as though with lasers. Rows of over-sized light bulbs, like those found in the library of Asgard, line the ceiling and cast the room in light so bright that it stings my eyes.

Why Nephilim would require such bright light is beyond me. Like other denizens of the underworld, they have grown accustomed to the dark. I fish around in one of my pouches and dig out my sunglasses. After putting them on, I check out the rest of the room.

Rows of large glass containers full of purple liquid line the walls. But that's not what's strangest about them. They appear to be attached to some kind of machine. A modern machine built of metal, each with a terminal that looks like…a computer, but far more modern than anything I saw in 1988—the year I was taken from the world outside. The size of the stations is also confusing. They look like they were built for humans.

Not humans, I realize.

Thinkers.

The thinkers are Nephilim who are renowned for tinkering with living things, and are apparently technologically advanced. While I haven't seen a thinker before, judging by the size of the terminals, they must be similar to the gatherers and seekers, whose lithe bodies, large egg-shaped heads and oval eyes give them an alien appearance.

The center of the room holds lines of tables, some large enough to hold a thirty foot Nephilim warrior. Some small enough for a human child. But all of them are just a few feet off the floor. And all of them have troughs running around the edges. *To siphon away blood*, I think. Operating tables.

This is a laboratory!

As I walk into the room, I see purple stains around many of the largest tables and around the drains in the floor. Several warriors recently went under the knife. But why? Nephilim are impervious to harm. For what reason would they need surgery? Knowing no answers would come from this line of questioning, I move deeper into the lab. To my left, the purple liquid-filled tanks grow smaller, as do the tables to my right. The space is very organized.

Thinkers, like human thinkers—scientists, doctors, philosophizers—appear to crave order on the level of someone with obsessive compulsive disorder. Everything about this place is in order. Symmetrical. Which I normally appreciate. When I was five, I had these flat wooden shapes. I sorted them by shape and color and arranged them into symmetrical patterns that my parents would tape together. I've always appreciated symmetry, but here, in the underworld, I find it unnerving.

Though not nearly as unnerving as what I see next. A body. It floats in one of the smaller purple tanks. I can't take my eyes away from it as I walk closer. It appears to be a child, free floating in the purple liquid, which I now realize must be diluted Nephilim blood. When an operation is complete, the subject, if needed, can be immersed in a bath of healing Nephilim blood. I look at the still form of the body inside the tank as it slowly rotates. Apparently, this one couldn't be saved by the blood of the Nephilim.

The body is upside down and spinning, like there's a gentle current in the tank. I can hear the whir of equipment working. There must be a filtration system in each tank, but they're efficient and well maintained. I can barely hear the sound. The face comes into view and I step back. The eyes are big and black, like a gatherer's. The body is skinny, also like a gatherer's, but that appears to be more from starvation than natural physiology. In fact, the ribcage and other bone structures appear to be human.

I look closer and gasp. While the face has the eyes and non-existent nose of a gatherer, it has human lips. They're pink and full in a way I recognize.

My parents call them Vincent lips.

My lips.

"No," I whisper. This is one of the failed attempts to duplicate me. "No…"

I spin around, looking at the other tanks. There are a few more on this wall holding bodies, but every single tank on the far wall is also full. Maybe fifty bodies. Fifty dead copies of me.

This is where Xin was created.

And Luca.

And the four other duplicates I have yet to meet.

As anger wells inside me, I turn to the far side of the room and find several surfaces covered with glass tubes, trays of surgical tools and odd-looking supplies whose function I can't possibly guess. But what I can see is that they're all neatly organized, waiting to be used by thinkers—Nephilim who have created and killed versions of me, again and again and again. I turn my anger toward their organized stations. I unclip Whipsnap and lash out. Glass shatters. Supplies fly through the air. My rage-filled shouts echo around me. Organization becomes chaos.

But while my vengeance is messy, it is far from satisfying.

That is, until I hear a shriek of despair.

I spin to face the newcomer who has just entered the lab from a small adjoining hallway. The figure is short for a Nephilim, about a foot shorter than me. Its body is concealed by a purple hooded cloak that also hides its face. But its head is the size of a large, egg-shaped watermelon.

Is this a thinker?

I steel my thoughts, preparing for a mental attack. I have no idea if the thinkers are capable of such a thing, but since the gatherers and seekers both can, I decide to ere on the side of caution.

But no mental attacks or communications come.

The thing just stands on the other side of the room, looking back and forth frantically at the destruction I've wrought. In fact, the thing doesn't seem to notice me at all until, still filled with anger, I pick up a glass bottle and smash it against the wall.

The thing's head snaps toward me. Then it starts walking in my direction. Walking is a generous word. It's more of a shamble. And it's speaking. Not to me. It's more of an angry muttering, like a grandmother tired of loud teenagers. The voice is high and sharp, mixed with the occasional growl. As it moves across the floor, it steps through fields of broken glass, which crunches beneath its feet. A trail of purple bloody footprints forms in its wake. The glass cuts the flesh, but this is a Nephilim. It's not only healing from the wounds quickly, but it's also enjoying the pain.

As I take a defensive stance, I feel a prick on my own foot. I glance down and realize that I'm surrounded by glass too. But if I cut myself, I won't be healing so quickly.

Clack, clack, clack. The thing reaches up and taps its fingertips across the top of a table as it walks past. The impacts sound hard, and I think the thing must have long hard fingernails. But when it closes to within twenty feet and taps its fingers on the next table, I get a look at the hand. Scalpel-like blades have been surgically inserted into each of the thing's six fingers. *Clack, clack, clack.* The muttering intensifies. The tapping grows louder. More irritated.

The small Nephilim is trying to intimidate me. And it's working.

"Stop!" I shout.

The thing's head twitches up slightly. I can feel the thing looking at my face, but its eyes are hidden in the stark shadow created by the bright overhead lights. I can see its mouth now, small, like a gatherer's, but full of little, almost needle-like, teeth. The mouth opens and lets out a laugh.

The fact that it finds me funny, aggravates me. I point the blade end of Whipsnap toward its head. Doesn't this Nephilim know who I am? What I'm capable of? Granted, I rejected Nephil, so I'm no longer his vessel, or the Lord of the Nephilim. But I am the guy strong enough to reject Nephil, who entered Tartarus and walked back out. I'm far from cocky, but I'm pretty sure that after my last display of power, even a warrior might be a little more cautious than this little thinker.

Which means it knows something that I don't.

Something that it finds funny.

Which I hate. And it seems to know that, because it giggles again.

Clack, clack, clack.

"Who are you?" I demand.

Clack, clack, clack.

When I get no answer, I sweep Whipsnap out in a wide arc, shattering more glass containers and knocking a tray of large-toothed saws to the floor.

The thing shrieks at me, all humor gone.

I ask again, "Who are you?"

It giggles again, this time more subdued. As I target another tabletop, the small Nephilim reaches up and takes hold of its cloak. The bladed fingertips slice into the thick fabric like it's not

even there. The hood peels back and the thing's face is fully revealed. With the horrible punch line to the thing's inside joke
revealed, it starts laughing again.

Then it attacks.

13

I have no powers.

My arm is injured.

I'm exhausted.

But none of these things are as dangerous to me right now as my distraction. It's the eyes. They're not big and oval and inhuman. They're mine.

This creature, like everything else in this lab, is part me.

Aimee tried to warm me about the other four living duplicates. She was surprised by Xin's actions, but held out no hope that the other four could be redeemed. And now, as I look into the light blue eyes that match mine, I see nothing but hatred. The tufts of stiff red hair growing from the prodigious head like stands of grass confirm its corruption. The sharp sting I feel as one of six razorblade fingertips traces a red line across my chest confirms its lethality.

The pain pulls me from my shocked state as the creature swipes at my gut, aiming to disgorge my innards. I block the strike with Whipsnap, spin into a crouch and after bending Whipsnap back, I let the mace end snap out. The strike is fluid, fast and as good as any hunter could achieve. And the results are better than the separate personalities of Ull and Solomon could hope for. Ull would have been all power and no direction. Solomon would have been on target, but lacking commitment. Whereas now, being whole, the blow is the best of both worlds.

The mace caves in the side of the thing's head. It slumps over, falling into the large-toothed saw blades, some of which dig into its flesh. A killing blow.

If it were human.

As the creature stirs, I remember the color of its blood. Purple. Nephilim. Unlike Xin, whose blood is red, and very human, this half-me is Nephilim through and through. Which not only means I have no problem killing it, despite it having my eyes, but also means completing the task will be quite difficult.

Before it's even fully healed, the thing lunges. Both bladed hands are outstretched and reaching for my legs. I have no doubt the razor fingers can sever flesh and bone, so I act quickly and defensively, leaping away. Before I land, I remember the broken glass on the floor. Using Whipsnap like a miniature pole-vaulting pole, I push the mace into the floor and shove myself atop a human-sized operating table.

As I roll over and push myself up, I hear skittering glass. The creature is giving chase. And fast. I get my feet under me and jump away just as the thing lands on the table, gouging its claws across the stone surface.

I land on my feet this time and turn to strike the creature as it leaps toward me. But the thing is frozen atop the first table, look-ing down at the twelve lines scraped into the otherwise perfectly smooth surface. Its body quakes. And then it screams. Its small chest heaves as its blue eyes lock onto mine.

The continued destruction of this perfect lab enrages the thinker creation. It must have been trained as a thinker, or at least to value order like a thinker. But it was left behind as a caretaker. Or guardian. And right now, it is failing.

With a shriek, the creature dives at me, but falls short and smashes into the side of the table I'm standing on. *Its anger makes it clumsy*, I realize.

I jump to another, slightly larger, stone operating table where a row of hammers—each designed for a specific task—is lined up along the edge. As the thing leaps back up to a table top, I snatch up a hammer, take aim and whip it toward the ceiling. A sharp crash resounds as the hammer finds its mark on the side of one of the large light bulbs. Thick glass rains down from above and the light winks out. Though the effect on the overall luminosity of the room is negligible, the mess is horrendous.

When the small me-thing cries out, I think that one of the glass shards has landed in its eye or something, but when I look, the creature is unharmed. Just really, really angry. A purple tinged foam oozes from its mouth. Then it speaks, shouting Sumerian obscenities that spray the purple like one of those automatic lawn sprinklers that move from one side to the other *tick, tick, tick, tick, pfffft, tick, tick tick.*

While it wails on, I look at its forehead, looking for the telltale pulse that reveals the Nephilim weak spot. When I don't see it, I have a kind of revelation. *Only the warriors wear the metal bands that protect their foreheads.* Which means the other races either don't have weak spots, or they're not nearly as invulnerable— perhaps they're far easier to kill. Which might also explain why the warriors are the ruling class.

Before the creature finishes fuming, I decide to press the attack. I leap forward and strike out with the blade end of Whipsnap. To say the little Nephilim is surprised, is an understatement. It bounds straight up into the air like it's got coiled springs for legs. But the leap is uncontrolled and off balance. The thing's body twists as it rises. When Whipsnap's blade slips through the air beneath the creature's body, it bites into the flesh of its arm and severs one of its six fingered hands.

An arc of purple blood sprays from the wrist as the thing spins and lands on the floor.

Moment of truth, I think, watching the thing spin, growl and gnash at everything around it like it's the Tasmanian Devil. When it finally stops and gets back to its feet, I see the hand. Or, rather, where the hand used to be. Instead of growing a new hand, like a warrior might, the wound has simply sealed over. My next thought is a little dark, but accurate: *dismemberment is the key.*

Once again, the small Nephilim isn't prepared for my attack. I suspect that while it was trained to obsess over details, cleanliness and organization, it wasn't taught how to fight. So far, it's been reacting from anger and instinct. Armed with the knowledge of how to kill this Nephilim, I now have the upper hand.

I almost feel bad for the thing as I leap to the floor next to it, careful to place my feet where there's no broken glass. It leaps at me, swiping desperately with its one remaining clawed hand. I lean back, easily dodging the strike. The creature spins in the air, pulled around by the momentum of its failed attack. As the thing rotates in the air, I consider sparing its life. It is, after all, partly me.

My logic is answered by emotion. With a shout, I bring Whipsnap's blade down and sever head from body. The two halves, which are nearly the same size, fall next to each other. The head rolls and spins, coming to rest against the base of a stone table. Purple blood pools around the separated parts, but nothing else happens. The creature is dead. And as a Nephilim, whose spirit cannot exist eternally outside of Tartarus, it ceases to exist. Which is for the best, I decide. They might have given it my eyes, but there was nothing else human about it.

With the thing dead at my feet, my interest in this Nephilim laboratory hits an all time low. It's not a safe or smart place to be, especially now that I've wrecked the place and left my scent all over it. It seems unlikely that anyone or anything will be returning to the lab, which was unaffected by the flood, but if a hunter comes to this place, they'll know I've been here. That I'm alive. And that I'm free from Tartarus.

And if that happens, I need to be as far away from this horrible place as I can be. I head for the large staircase and glance to the left, looking at one of the largest of the liquid filled tubes. It's nearly fifteen feet tall, and it's occupied. The shape inside makes me pause.

It's not human. For a moment, I mistake it for one of the

oversized centipedes, but it's not even a body.

It's a body *part*, the likes of which I have only ever seen once.

In Tartarus.

Cronus's tail.

The long, scorpion-like tail and stinger are impossible to mistake. For a moment, I'm filled with dread. Did Cronus trick me? Was he captured and experimented on? Both of these concerns are quickly discounted. Cronus couldn't have been taken here, dismantled and pickled before I got here. The timing is all off and the scent of his blood would still hang in the air. This place hasn't been used in sometime.

The tail belongs to someone else.

Or, like all of my dead duplicates, it was grown here. But for what purpose?

A question for another day, I decide. But I can't let this appendage be used for anything sinister, so I climb up on top of one of the Nephilim-sized operating tables and whack the glass with Whipsnap's mace. The cylinder shatters, spilling gouts of purple fluid, and the tail, onto the floor.

As the liquid spreads toward the staircase, I leap from tabletop to tabletop. I beat the purple fluid to the staircase by a few feet, and as I start down the stairs, the trickling sound of flowing liquid gives chase. I quickly reach the crack through which I entered the smooth tunnel and slip back into the craggy, rough underworld. As I backtrack through the tunnel, I feel calmer, more in control, but the disturbing discoveries I made in the lab haunt me like specters.

14

I head up through the underground as quickly as I can. Not just because I want to reach the surface, but because I know time moves more slowly the deeper you are. If I linger in the depths too long, the conflict on the surface will flash past before my arrival. There is no rhyme or reason to my path; I'm just heading up. But after miles of walking, it happens. I recognize a tunnel. I'm not far from New Jericho. And from there, it's an easy trek to the surface and then…Clark Station 1? Clark Station 2?

Part of me says this is a very bad idea. My nostalgia has made me predictable before. Its how Ninnis found me. It's also what led to Tobias's death. I might walk into a trap. That said, no one knows I'm here. Ninnis and the Nephilim, if they're even still on Antarctica, won't be looking for me. And both Em and Kainda are smart enough to not return to those places. Not for long anyway. But maybe long enough to leave a clue. It's the only starting place I have that might help me find my friends, and help. As much as I'd like to finish my journey, and fight, without endangering anyone else I care about, it's just not possible. I need help.

To find the Jericho Shofar, I first need to locate Hades. But I have no idea where to find him. I assume he resides at the Olympus citadel, like the other faux-Olympian-god Nephilim, but I've never been there. I need a guide. And without my powers, I'll need back-up. Significant back-up. I was able to kill Ull using my powers, but I'm fairly certain such a thing won't be possible without them. Even with Em and Kainda fighting with me, I doubt we could manage to slay even one of the warriors.

But this is my fate, so I strike out for New Jericho, and for the surface. My thoughts drift to Pilgrim's Progress. Christian faced trials along his path, and accepted aid from others to overcome those trials. But the pearly gates that were his ultimate destination are a far cry from the bloodshed that likely waits at the end of my path. Still, I see no alternative and continue on the path laid out before me, which for now, leads ever upward.

Several hours later, I'm standing at the top of what was once a three hundred foot waterfall. I jumped from its ledge to escape the hunter, Preeg. Using my control over the wind, I slowed my fall and survived. Preeg gave chase and died on impact. If I were to make the same leap now, without my powers, I would share his fate. That is, if the massive chamber containing the ruins of New Jericho weren't flooded. The three hundred foot drop to the water's surface has been reduced to twenty. Not even the tallest temple of New Jericho is visible. While I'm happy to not have to walk through the ruins and past the statue and gravesite of my former master, the Nephilim known as Ull, this also puts a damper in my plans. The tunnel I had planned to take to the surface is now under hundreds of feet of water.

A distant roar reminds me that there is a waterfall on the other side of the chamber. By the sound of it, it's pumping more water than ever before. The cliff edge I'm standing on was also a waterfall at one time, but it's now dry, its water source either gone or redirected. The flooding must be coming primarily from the other waterfall, which is fed by melt water from the surface.

That's a lot of melted water.

Stealing myself for the cold water, I dive into the lake. I arch my body and return quickly to the surface, taking fast, shallow breaths. There was a time when it took me twenty minutes to jump into a pool in the middle of the summer. And when I did, I would holler about how cold the water felt. *Swim*, my father would tell me, *kick your legs and you'll warm up.* I never listened. I would dog paddle to the ladder, yank myself out, wrap up in a towel and help myself to potato chips and a Coke like they were a reward earned in battle. But I take his advice now. I point myself in the right direction, and swim for all I'm worth.

When I reach the other side, I'm exhausted. Few things wear the body down like a long swim. And I can't stay in the water. Treading water will only make me more tired, and if I lose consciousness, I could slip beneath the surface and drown. But the only escape is the waterfall. And it rages.

Undeterred, I swim around the water pouring out of the gap in the solid stone wall. The surface is smooth and slick with moisture. Even the strongest hunter couldn't climb this surface—

that is, unless, they have climbing claws capable of clinging to the minutest blemishes in the stone. I put the climbing claws on my hands, reach up and drag the first one down against the stone until it catches on something. I yank myself up, all of my weight pulling on that one arm and the feeder teeth. Luckily, the Nephilim have strong bones, and my conditioned arms, while tired, are up to the task.

The rest of my body, however, is straining. The shallow incision across my chest, given to me by the now dead thinker abomination, stings sharply with every twitch of muscle. The wound scabbed over quickly, so I never gave it much attention. The intense pain makes me think I should have. The sealed wound has been soaking in the lake water. It might have reopened when I was swimming. Could be deeper than I first thought too.

Later, I tell myself. Right now, I have to climb.

I pull myself up the wall slowly, dragging the claws, finding a hold and pulling myself up again and again until I've covered fifty feet. The pain in my chest is intense, but I can't let it distract me now. I'm focused. Determined. And possibly, at a dead end.

The waterfall roars to my left. There is no ledge to step on and entering the water here is impossible. The strong current would yank me back into the lake and I lack the strength to repeat the climb. I scuttle across the wall, clinging to it with the climbing claws, and maneuver myself so I'm above the waterline. As I round the bend into the tunnel, I find footholds big enough for my toes and moving becomes easier. A few minutes later, I'm free of the wall, standing on the shore of a river that is at least ten feet deeper than I remember.

I turn my head up river and smell, searching the air for signs of life, human or otherwise. At first, I detect nothing. No blood. No rot. Nothing.

But then, there's something faint. Something out of place. It's earthy, but not stone. It's more like dirt. Like soil. Damp and fragrant.

Like *spring*.

I close my eyes and breathe deeply. A blanket of air rushes past, pushed by the river. It carries the scent of vegetation, flowers and water. It smells like...life. And then I feel it.

The air.

It's warm.

15

To say I'm confused is an understatement. The air flowing through this tunnel should be icy cold. Granted, I couldn't feel the temperature during my previous time here, but the science—

My eyes pop open as I remember the cause. When I bonded with Nephil, he reached out and became bonded with the Earth. The bond lasted just a moment, but it was long enough for him to reposition Antarctica at the equator. Billions died. I sensed it. But I hoped it wasn't true. But now there can be no doubt. The world has been remade. Antarktos has thawed under an equatorial sun. It explains the flooding. The air. The smell. And the disappearance of most subterranean species.

They've headed to the surface.

Back to the surface.

Most of the creatures eking out a living in the underground were originally surface dwellers. Like the Nephilim, when the continent froze, they moved beneath the surface. If not for the strange properties of this continent, they would have most likely died out long ago. But they are once again enjoying their time in the sun.

The sun.

I haven't seen it in years. And as I head for the surface, following tunnels I know well, I'm filled with a sense of dread. The feeling is similar to what I felt when I was first dragged underground by Ninnis. The surface is an unfamiliar world now, even more so now that the snow is melting.

When I reach the final tunnel leading outside, I pause. There's the crack where I hid the Polaroid photo of Mira and me. Not far away is the section of wall upon which I carved the words, "I forgive you," for Ninnis. The words are illegible now, scratched away, most likely by Ninnis himself. Up ahead is the tunnel exit through which I would normally see a deep blue sky. Now the sky is full of thick, dark clouds. Thunderheads. The kind you see in New England in late spring.

The scent of ozone lingers in the air. Lightning, I think, just before the sky flickers with a brilliance that makes me shout in pain. The dark clouds had made the light of day bearable, but the sudden flash is as bright as the sun. I clench my eyes shut, holding my hands over them, and I see the bright green image of a lightning streak as though it's etched into my eyelids.

Everything about my return to the surface feels awful. That is, until the booming thunder rolls past, vibrating the ground beneath me. It's like Behemoth has just fallen down next to me. The power in that rumble brings a smile to my face. I used to lie on my bed and watch thunderstorms, as they swept past and out to sea. I've missed them.

After donning my sunglasses, I inch toward the surface. I'm sure I look like a fool—a long haired, Tarzan-like, bearded tee-nager wearing sunglasses. But unlike during my years in school, there will be no one around to point out my ridiculous state. As I near the end of the tunnel, light fills the sky again. I squint against the light, but the dark sunglasses take the edge off.

Even with the cloud cover, when I step out of the tunnel, the daylight hurts. I close my eyes as I step out into the world. The first thing I notice is the land beneath my feet. It's soft and squishy, like the remains of some dead creature. Through squinted eyes, I look down and see a dark goop pushing up between my toes.

Mud.

I crouch and scoop some of the soft earth into my hand. The grainy wetness feels similar to the insides of a centipede. I bring it to my nose and inhale slowly and deeply. The scent triggers memories. Playing in the back yard with Justin. Gardening with my mom. Exploring a swamp with my father.

I wasn't dreading the surface. I was dreading the memories a thawed Antarctica would bring. Just the smell of mud is potent enough to send me back in time. It's not that I don't want to remember, or that the memories are bad, it's that they hurt. I've been here for more than twenty years, even though from my perspective it's been closer to three. I can't return to the life I knew. It's gone for good and now, thanks to Nephil's reposition-ing of the world, potentially destroyed. My parents could be dead. And if I give these things any attention, I will enter my own personal Slough of Despond.

I flick the mud off my hand and stand up. My eyes slowly acclimate to the sunglass-darkened, cloud-dimmed daylight. I look up and find the world remade.

Where a glacier once slid slowly into the ocean, there is now a lush, green valley. A variety of tall trees, few of which I recognize, cover the land. The barren, frozen dessert of Antarctica is now a thick, green jungle.

How is this possible? I think. Cronus said I'd been away for just three months. And my time in the deep underworld was brief. It couldn't have added more than a few more weeks. These trees couldn't have sprung up so quickly. This looks more like twenty years worth of growth!

Have I been gone for another twenty years? My stomach twists at the idea. Not only would my parents certainly be dead, but the outside world would have been dominated by the Nephilim long ago. Em, Kainda and Luca will all be adults, if they're even still alive.

Don't get distracted, I tell myself. *You don't have the answers. Stay out of the Slough.*

I step into the jungle, heading downhill to where Clark Station 2 once stood. The thick canopy of large leaves far above is a relief. It blocks out so much of the light that I'm able to take off my sunglasses. It's almost like the underground, but above the ground. As my eyes continue to adjust, my senses that are unaffected by light, take in my surroundings. The smell of earthy decay reaches me first, and then the scent of animals, some familiar, some new. But there is no doubt that the denizens of the subterranean world now inhabit the surface. If the smell alone didn't convince me, the sounds permeating the jungle would have. Though I have yet to see a living creature, I can hear them loud and clear. A crestie barks in the distance. Other creatures call out warnings as the hunt plays out. All around, I hear birds.

There were no birds in the underworld, so where did they come from? I've read that birds can sense things like volcanic eruptions and earthquakes, just before they strike. The birds take to the sky. If the same thing happened when the Earth's crust shifted, it's possible that the world slipped by beneath the airborne birds and they found themselves transported to a new continent. I know my theory is sound when the distinct red, blue and yellow plumage of a macaw flaps past overhead. The bird is a native of Brazil. It must feel right at home in this new rainforest.

Advancing carefully and quietly, I move down the grade, deeper into the forest, where the trees grow to impossible heights that could easily conceal an army of Nephilim. When I've covered the precise distance between the cave exit and Clark Station 2, I stop. There's a tree where the metal hanger-like station should be.

I creep forward. Maybe the land has changed? Maybe it was pulled away by ice as it flowed out to sea. It seems unlikely, because ice melted by the sun would melt from the top down and the buried structure would have been freed from it slowly and gently.

Whump-bump.

The ground beneath my feet bubbles down under my weight and springs back up when I step off. I've stepped on something. Falling to my knees, I quickly brush away a layer of detritus and several inches of soil. When I'm done, I stare at my discovery. It's a metal panel, ridged like the surface of Clark Station 2. Was it buried again? I wonder. But I quickly find the outer edges and lift the rusted metal from the ground.

A quick search of the surrounding area reveals more of the same. Clark Station 2 has been destroyed. There's nothing left.

Sadness grips me. I'm not sure what I expected to find here. Maybe comfort in the familiar, or…the note. I'd forgotten about Mira's note, but some part of me must have hoped to find it. But it's long gone now, like Mira herself.

My thoughts turn to Clark Station 1. It's just five miles from here. Not only is it the place of my birth, but it was also home to Luca, Em and Tobias for a time. If there are any clues to their location to be found, they'll be there.

Moving fast, I begin a reckless charge through the jungle that will get me to Clark Station 1 in thirty minutes. I'm noisy and leaving a path that is easy to follow. Like I said, reckless. I already knew there are cresties hunting nearby. What I didn't know was that a different sort of hunter now stalked the jungle—one equally as deadly as the ancient dinosaurs.

16

The man is as surprised by me, as I am by him. He spins around with wide eyes, like a child caught stealing cookies. His complexion and facial features look Arab, and his clothing is modern military—fatigues, boots and weapons. He's got some kind of automatic weapon slung over his back and a handgun on his hip.

I didn't see the man crouched by a tree and nearly bowled right into him. But my reflexes are fast and I lunge to the side, avoiding a collision that would have been painful. I roll back to my feet and spin toward the man with open hands—what I hope is still universal for "I mean you no harm."

Unfortunately, he's not of the same mind. When his hand comes up, it's holding a handgun. He aims it at my chest, but doesn't pull the trigger. He's no doubt confused by the half-naked teenager standing before him. In all my time below ground, I never felt self-conscious about my scant clothing. Everyone underground dressed like this. Survival depended on it. But under this man's bewildered gaze, I'm feeling wholly underdressed.

His eyes linger on the sharp blade and spiked mace attached to either side of my waist where Whipsnap is clipped.

"I'm not going to hurt you," I say.

Something about my words enrages the man. I can only understand one word of his reply. "American." And it sounds more like an accusation than a question. What has happened in the world that the first person I come across wants to kill me because I'm an American?

Rather than tempting fate, I shake my head, no, and say, "Antarctican."

He seems to understand what I'm saying. Antarctica is Antarctica in any language. But as expected, the claim makes no sense to the man. With no way to elaborate verbally, I motion to my lack of clothing and repeat, "Antarctican." I point to the earth beneath my feet. "Underground."

Again, I think he understands because his face screws up like he's just stepped in cresty dung.

He shouts a long string of words I can't understand. I don't know if he's telling me to do something, telling me I'm an idiot or performing last rights before shooting me in the head. When I don't react, he takes a step closer and waggles the gun angrily in my face. "Knees!" he says.

That, I understand. He wants me on my knees. And as fast as I am, I can't outrun a bullet. With no powers to assist me, I have no choice but to comply. I drop to my knees, hands still raised.

He puts a hand to the back of his head, pantomiming what he wants me to do and shouts, "Hands!"

I place my hands behind my head and lock my fingers together.

I'm not sure if I'm being taken prisoner, or if I'm about to be executed. I'm not even sure what this man is doing here. His presence is an enigma. If twenty more years had passed, and the outside world had been dominated, then there would be no way this man could be here. And he can't be part of any kind of resistance, not with those weapons. Given his surprise by my appearance, I'd guess that he, and the world at large, has yet to encounter the Nephilim or even a single hunter.

There's still time, I think. The sudden growth of this rainforest is a mystery, but no more strange than the half-human, half-demon monsters aiming to wipe humanity from the globe. If only I had a way to explain all this to the man. We're on the same side. He just doesn't know it yet!

With the gun aimed at my face, he steps closer. I feel uncomfortable staring into the barrel of the weapon. I cast my eyes downward. That's when I see what the man was doing by the tree. There's a grenade tied to the tree. The pin keeping it from detonating is attached to a taut wire stretched across the ground, and it's tied to a second tree. The wire is only partially covered with leaf litter. The man must have been covering it when I showed up.

He shouts something at me, drawing my eyes back up. He's leaning down, reaching out for Whipsnap. The gun is just inches from my face. He takes hold of the weapon—and tugs. He's totally unprepared when Whipsnap detaches from my belt and springs to life in his hand. He stumbles backward and squeezes off a shot. The round zips over my head, but I don't give it a second thought. Once the man recovers from his surprise, I have no doubt he's going to shoot me.

I charge forward as the man brings the gun back down. When the barrel comes level with my face, I take hold of his hand and push up while ducking my head to the side. The second shot misses, but the violent report in my ear stuns me for a moment. The man takes advantage of my disorientation and whacks me in the side with Whipsnap.

Thankfully, the man has no idea how to wield the weapon of my creation properly and the blow is nothing more than a gentle thump. I keep the gun at bay with my left hand and take hold of Whipsnap's shaft with my right. This might normally become a contest of strength, but I know my weapon, and despite the man's tight grasp, I'm able to use it against him. With a quick twist and pull, the top end of Whipsnap bends. Careful not to use crushing force, I bring the mace down on the man's head.

His grip on Whipsnap falls away. The gun falls to the ground, followed by the man. He's not unconscious, but he's stunned. He shakes his head and blinks his eyes. When blood trickles over his forehead, he reaches up and feels the wound, wincing as he touches it. His confusion melts to rage as he screams at me.

"Please!" I shout back, raising a single open hand to the man. "I don't want to hurt you!"

But the man is beyond reason, even if he could understand what I'm saying. He reaches over his shoulder and starts to pull around his automatic weapon. If I allow him to do that, I'm a dead man. But what can I do? I don't want to kill a human being. I don't know if I could live with myself. A harder strike with either end of Whipsnap would kill the man. Then I remember

my other weapons, ones I rarely have a need for when I've got
Whipsnap.

I jump forward and punch the man hard in his face. Pain radiates up my arm, but the effect on him is much worse. He
slumps to the ground, unmoving. I stand over him breathing
heavily.

Why? I think. *Why would this man want to kill me?* He didn't
know who I am. Didn't recognize me personally, or as anything
that could be explained by his worldview. But here he is, armed
for war, laying traps and ready to murder a perfect stranger. It's
just as twisted as anything I encountered during my time underground, but it makes less sense.

This is not the homecoming I had hoped for.

I take the man's weapons and look them over. I don't recognize the handgun, but the rifle is an AK-47. I consider keeping
the weapons, but they don't feel right. They're designed for killing people, not Nephilim, and could only be useful in the hands
of a skilled marksman, which I am not. Not with modern weapons anyway. Tobias trained me on his bow a few times, and I
was pretty good, but that was when I had the wind to assist my
aim. I toss the weapons into the jungle in different directions.
Removing the man's weapons might be a death sentence, but I
won't be the one killing him. And I won't have to wonder if he's
killed anyone else. I carefully cut the grenade free from the tree
and wind up to toss it, but pause, wondering if I should keep it.
While a gun won't be effective against a Nephilim, a grenade
could certainly do some damage. At least temporarily. But I've

never used a grenade, and I have no idea how long it would take to explode. It's being used with a tripwire, so maybe this variety detonates once the pin is pulled? With no way to find out, I decide to err on the side of safety and toss the grenade away.

I search the man's body and find a knife, which is duller than mine, so I toss it. I'm surprised that he's not carrying any other grenades. Then it occurs to me that he probably was carrying more grenades. There might be tripwires set up all through the jungle.

Going to have to be more careful, I think, and I look around me for anything that looks like a concealed wire. Finding nothing, I search the man's pockets. He's got a canteen of water and some dehydrated food supplies. Enough for just a few days, which makes me think he's not alone out here, or he's stashed the rest of his gear some place else. In his breast pocket, I find a folded piece of paper.

I unfold the paper. It expands to the size of a poster. In fact, it looks a lot like the poster of Antarctica that hung on my bedroom wall before Justin and I coated it in volcanic red dye. I can't read the words. They're all in Arabic, but the South Pole has been flagged.

Is this man traveling to the South Pole? He doesn't seem like any explorer I've ever heard of. He's more military than anything. After folding up the map, I place it in a belt pouch, return Whipsnap to my waist and without a second glance back at the unconscious man, resume my trek toward Clark Station 1, only much more slowly, and much more carefully.

I arrive fifteen minutes later and despite finding the place of my birth still standing, I also find it inhabited. And the squatters are decidedly not happy to see me.

17

Eight heads crane around in my direction. Fifteen black eyes stare at me, waiting for me to move. The one with a missing eye steps to the front of the pack, his head poking forward with each step. Brave for a turkuin, I think. The name 'turkuin' is my own. I've eaten three of them over the past years, and they're pretty tasty, but they're also rare in the underground. They're skittish, running at the slightest hint of odor or shift in the breeze. That the one-eyed male, the largest of the bunch, is staring me down is strange.

Turkuins are, as my oh-so-creative name insinuates, something like a cross between a turkey and a penguin—on steroids. Their bodies are covered in tightly bunched, small feathers—white in the front and black in the back. They also have long, bright orange feathers over their eyes that wrap around the sides of their heads like some kind of sci-fi movie mascara. They're usually about three feet tall, but they have powerful legs that make them fast, and sharp claws that make them dangerous. Their hooked beaks are also quite sharp. But turkuins are not at all aggressive.

Until now.

The male bobs his head and takes another step toward me. He's acting like a male ostrich protecting his harem. The orange feathers over his eyes and on the side of his head flare out. He's trying to intimidate me.

Me. A hunter.

Turkuins are normally skittish, but if they get a whiff of—or see—a hunter, they squawk in panic, bolting in whatever direction they're facing. It's the easiest way to catch them. Just jump out and watch as one inevitably careens into a wall and knocks itself silly.

So why is this turkuin not panicking? More than that, why does old one-eye here look like he's about to attack me?

"I'd like to leave you alone," I say to one-eye, "but I need to have a look inside." The birds have built a nesting area inside Clark Station 1, gaining entrance through a large rusted out hole where the front door used to be.

I take hold of Whipsnap and pull. It springs open in my hand. The sudden appearance of a weapon should have been enough to sap the bird's bravery, but it just stops for a moment, rotates its head back and forth and blinks its lone eye at me. Then it steps forward again and lets out a squawk that is nearly a growl. The feathers on its head shake and rattle. The seven other birds fan out and join the hunt.

I nearly laugh. The outside world equivalent might be a pack of snarling Chihuahuas. Then again, a pack of Chihuahuas could probably get in a few good bites. And these birds' beaks are sharp enough to take off a finger or take a scoop out of an arm, never mind their claws, or the fact that I've never actually seen them fight. I'm not sure what to expect.

The predatory pack lowers their heads like stalking cats.

I shout, "Heeya! Heeya!" and shake Whipsnap at them.

Eight sets of orange feathers flare out and shake. It's a rather spectacular display, the purpose of which still eludes me, that is, until they attack. The vibrant feathers held my gaze for just a moment, but it was long enough for me not to see the muscles in their legs coil. All eight birds rush me as one unit. One-eye leads the charge, followed by four on the ground. The other three leap into the air, flapping their feeble wings hard enough to carry them the distance to me.

The sudden and coordinated attack surprises me. I flinch and stumble back, nearly tripping over the ground. Clumsy!

In the moment before the birds reach me, I decide that for some reason I can't fathom, these creatures either aren't recognizing me as a hunter, or they have somehow forgotten why they feared hunters in the first place. Perhaps they're inspired by the jungle setting. Or the very different magnetic field at the equator. The reason why they're no longer afraid of a hunter isn't important. What *is* important is that I give them a reason to fear one now.

As one-eye reaches me, he stabs out with his beak, but thanks to the one eye, his depth perception is all screwed up and he pecks the air a foot in front of me. I sidestep and bring Whipsnap's blade down like a guillotine. One-eye's head falls to the ground, stopping the other turkuins in their tracks. The three in the air spasm and fall ungracefully to the ground.

One-eye's headless body keeps right on running until it smacks into a tree and flops over. The legs continue moving, spinning the body in rapid circles and spraying blood like a spin art toy. As the body slows to a twitchy stop, I calmly turn my head back to the flock. Their flared feathers fold slowly down. The birds lean their heads away from me, and take a few careful backward steps.

"Heeya!" I shout and the birds explode into a panicked retreat, squawking as they smash through the underbrush and disappear into the jungle.

"Well, one-eye," I say, looking down at the severed head. "You kind of brought that on yourself. But don't worry; I won't let you go to waste." I pick up the now motionless turkuin body and carry it to the entryway of Clark Station 1. The bird isn't that heavy, maybe forty pounds, but when I place it on the ground next to the rusted out hole, I feel exhausted.

I lean against the metal wall and catch my breath. I'm soaked with sweat, too. A cold drip strikes my shoulder. It's followed by another. And another. That's when I notice a loud hiss from above. The hiss grows louder by the moment. I turn toward the source of the sound and see the canopy shaking. The hiss grows louder still, but is then drowned out by a massive boom.

The storm has arrived.

And suddenly, it's on top of me.

The rainwater strikes the canopy first, filtering down to the forest floor as waterfalls pour from large leaves. The already dim forest floor grows darker. It's as though night has fallen in the middle of the day.

I put my head under a nearby trickle of water falling from above and catch some of it in my mouth. After drinking several mouthfuls, I retrieve one-eye's corpse and enter the dry interior of Clark Station 1. I'll need to skin and gut one-eye before I can cook and dry his flesh, all of which I can do fairly rapidly, but that can wait. Right now, I need to search for clues.

Clark Station 1 is in shambles. The first few rooms are missing walls. The contents of the rooms are wet and rotting, or rusted. Brightly colored splotches of mold cover nearly everything. Tobias's room is non-existent, any trace of him is destroyed. There are bits of cloth here and there—the remnants of what the turkuins didn't use to create their nests. Em's room is the same. The room I lived in during my stay with my adopted family has a large hole in the ceiling through which gouts of rain now pour, and have done so several times in the past. A layer of foul smelling sludge coats the floor.

I'm about to give up when I notice a closed door. Luca's room. If the door has remained closed all this time, the rot might be far less. I rush to the door, take hold of the handle and yank. Not only does the door open, but it also breaks free. My momentum pulls me back and I fall, taking the door with me. As I lay on the floor, bracing the door above my head, I realize I've made a few clumsy errors recently.

With my connection to the continent gone, am I becoming my old clumsy self again?

Pushing the door away takes some effort and I realize what's happening. I'm tired. Really tired. Strangely tired.

I'll sleep, I decide, *when I'm done with my search.*

My legs shake as I stand, and I frown. *What's happening to me?*

Pushing past my growing exhaustion, I stumble into the room, bracing myself against the wall. There's no hole in the ceiling, no water on the floor and no mold anywhere. Luca's room has been spared. Not for much longer now that I've pulled the door off, but long enough for me to find a clue about where the others are, if there is even a clue to be found.

Despite the lack of rot, the room is in shambles, like there was a fight. The small desk is broken and tipped over. Luca's rock collection is strewn on the floor. And the blankets from his bed dangle from where they snagged a screw in the wall.

This is where they found him, I think. While Ninnis and Kainda were busy killing Tobias and maiming Em and me, two other hunters, Preeg and Pyke, kidnapped Luca. They must have found him here. And he put up a fight. He might be my duplicate physically, but he's far tougher than I was at his age. I would have likely wilted in the face of danger and passed out like one of those fainting goats.

A chill starts in my legs and works its way up, spreading goose bumps over my skin. When it hits my stomach, it swirls with nausea. Then the chill moves up, spreads out to my arms and is gone.

What the…

My physical condition distracts me for just a moment. That's when I look at Luca's small bed. It was built from the homemade metal crib I slept in as a newborn baby. The mattress is old and flattened, but I know it hides something important. I lift the mattress up and find Luca's drawings and a single crayon hidden inside an old, large Ziploc bag. Tobias never saw these pictures. Each one is a sketch of some event that Luca witnessed through my eyes. The image on top is easily recognizable. Despite it being a child's drawing, the Nephilim with an arrow in his forehead is obviously Ull. One of my better moments.

A second chill rips up through my body. This time it is followed by a sharp pain in my chest. I pitch forward with a moan and grit my teeth against the ache.

What is happening to me?

It's a question I can no longer ignore, and I'm pretty sure there is nothing to find here. I stuff the sealed drawings into a pouch, and then look down to where the pain still burns on my chest.

What I see sucks the air from my lungs. The skin around the single razor thin wound across my chest it bright pink. But it's the yellow puss oozing from the wound that makes me cringe.

Had I still been underground I would kill a centipede, pry open the wound, stuff the goopy flesh inside the wound and wait for it to do its thing. But out here, in a jungle filled with unrecognizable plants, I'd be as likely to do more harm than good.

I could be back underground and possibly hunt down a centipede in the next two hours, but the chills are almost constant now, and I now know the sweat is from a fever. I won't be going anywhere. My body is going to have to handle this infection on its own. After removing Whipsnap from my waist, I climb up into the small bed, yank the blanket down from the wall and curl up into a fetal position. I look up at the ceiling and remember the last time I saw this view. It was the day we left Antarctica. My parents woke me up with soft cooing voices.

"Solomon," my mother said, though it was more like she was singing my name, "It's time to go home."

"I am home," I reply to the memory, somehow giving voice to the emotions I felt at the time. "Antarktos is my home. Don't make me leave."

When my father picks me up, I start crying. I don't want to leave.

"Are you ever going to let me hold you without crying?" my father asks with a chuckle.

"Give him to Aimee," my mother says. "He adores her."

I cried louder, somehow knowing it would be the last time I saw this room. And while my baby-self was mistaken, I remember my sorrow keenly. The memory becomes a dream as I slip into a deep, defenseless sleep.

18

I used to have dreams about falling. From the sides of buildings. From airplanes. From cliffs. I would fall, screaming, but I would never actually land. Instead, I would wake at the last possible moment. But the strangeness always continued because I would jolt in the bed like I'd actually just fallen—not from a cliff mind you, but at least a couple inches off the mattress. I often wondered if I'd actually somehow levitated. Had I known about my abilities then, I might have believed it was possible.

But this dream is nothing like that. I'm not sure where my fall began. I'm high. Really high. So I must have fallen out of an airplane or a space shuttle, because I can see Antarctica. The whole continent—green, but recognizable by its shape. As it occurs to me that I must actually be in space, I'm suddenly falling through the atmosphere. Clouds obscure my view. They're heavy with rain and they shimmer with light.

I pass through the storm as streaks of hot lightning flash past. Thunder booms instantaneously, shaking my body and drowning out my screams. Cold water pelts my body. Hail follows, so thick that it feels like I'm being punched all over. Something about the storm feels familiar.

You found me, I think, but I'm not sure who I'm talking to.

Then I'm through the clouds and the land below is revealed. It looks like an aerial view of the Brazilian rainforest, stretching as far as I can see. I streak down to meet the ground. This is where I'd normally wake up. But my fall becomes suspended, as though the wind is buffeting me.

Am I flying? I wonder, as the land passes by below.

A gray streak catches my eye and soon I'm passing over it.

It's a wall. The ruins of a very tall, stone wall. A Nephilim sized wall.

Before I can ruminate on the appearance of the wall, I'm beyond it. A river twists through the jungle beneath me, flowing in the opposite direction, toward the coast. The river ends at a massive lake, beyond which I see mountains, but I don't get a good look because I'm falling again.

A voice cuts through the wind rushing by my ears. The single word is distant, but shouted. "Soooolomoooon."

My descent is angled toward the far shore. I'm going to miss the water entirely.

"Soooooolomoooon!"

Who is that?

"Over here!"

The voice is closer now. Familiar.

There's a small beach on the shoreline. I see a small body standing on it, arms waving madly. "Sol! I'm here! I'm right he—"

I gasp, flail and fall out of the small bed.

Pain stabs my eyes. It's bright! I turn myself over, covering my head and fish for my sunglasses. Once I get them on, I sit up and take in my surroundings. I'm still in Luca's bedroom, which was mine when I was an infant. But a lot has changed. For starters, the roof is missing. I can tell the storm is gone because the leaves overhead glow bright green under the sun's gaze. I turn away from the view above, because it stings my eyes, even through the dark lenses.

The room is a disaster. It looked rummaged through before. Now it looks like a hurricane tore through. Everything is wet. I'm lying in a few inches of water. And there are little white golf balls everywhere.

Hail.

The storm.

"You found me," I say, remembering the dream.

I look up through the torn open roof. Was the storm really here because of me? The answer is strangely obvious.

Yes.

The storm came when I was born.

It came again upon my return to the continent.

And now, it greets me again as I rise from Tartarus.

But what does it mean?

I push myself up and wince. The pain in my chest is sharp. I glance down and see that the yellow puss is now gone, perhaps washed away by the rain I apparently slept through. But my skin is still red, and sore, and though I'm rested, I still feel quite weak.

Despite my far-from-perfect condition, the subject doesn't

hold my attention for long. I feel my mind pulled between the strangeness of the storm and the meaning of my dream. But I don't get to ponder either line of thought, because I'm not alone. A man screams, his voice a mixture of vitriol and fear. And happily, the sound is not directed at me.

When a squawk answers the shout, I know who the man is screaming at. I find Whipsnap on the floor next to me, pick it up and lean out the door. Looking down the ruined hallway toward the main living area where the rusted out door was previously—the whole side of the building is now missing—I see the Arab man. He wields a broken branch like a club, swinging it in wide circles to keep the seven turkuins away. They no doubt returned to find their nesting grounds in ruins and another person—not a hunter this time—taking shelter from the storm next to the corpse of their former pack leader.

Both sides of this fight have tried to kill me. I'm almost resigned to let it play out. I'd already determined that the man would have to survive on his own. But letting the man be eaten right in front of me... It's not right.

With a sigh, I step out of the room and head for the ruined living area. Neither the man, nor the predatory birds hear me coming, so when I clear my throat and all eight of them shriek in surprise, I can't help but smile. The turkuins react as they should, by squawking in fright, turning a quick one-eighty and bolting in a straight line. Five of them escape unharmed. One slams head first into a metal wall and snaps its neck. Another impales itself on the sharp end of a broken chair leg. It squawks in pain, trying to free itself.

Seeing the creature is dying and suffering, I walk toward it. Despite its perilous situation, the bird attempts to peck me with its sharp beak when I get close. As it strikes out at me, I catch its neck and give it a hard yank. Its life ends in a quick, painless crack. When I let go, the head flops to the side.

I turn to the man. His eyes are wide. He looks at the crude club in his hands, and then to Whipsnap. He backs away, no doubt remembering how I defeated him when he was armed with modern weapons.

I feel pity for the terrified man as he shuffles out of the ruined structure. I decide to give him a knife. Maybe he'll have a fighting chance. It's the least I can do for a man who tried to put a bullet in my head. "Wait," I say. "Hold on."

The man screams in response and takes off into the jungle. I'm about to give chase when a much more familiar call rips through the jungle. It's a cresty. A big one by the sound of it. More sounds follow. Snapping branches. Heavy foot falls.

When the Arab screams again, it's a pitch I'm not sure I've ever heard a man reach before.

The cresty roars again. The hunt is on.

And I know it will end quickly.

I also know that there's nothing I can do to help the man. Without my abilities, I wouldn't fare much better against a full-grown cresty than Kainda did. And cresties hunt in packs. The only thing I can do is wait for the feeding to begin and then head in the opposite direction.

But the hunt ends long before the cresties catch the man. An explosion tears through the jungle. The man must have triggered his own tripwire. I'm sorry the man died, but being blown to bits is a merciful death compared to being eaten alive. Unfortunately, it creates a problem for me. The man's shredded body might dissuade the cresties from eating it. They prefer to kill their prey—not have it blown to bits. The explosion most likely turned them away as well.

The hunt will continue.

I duck out of Clark Station 1, turn right and sprint. There are turkuins, tripwires, armed men, cresties and who knows what else lurking in the jungle, but if I don't put some distance between me and the cresties that I know for sure are behind me, they'll catch my scent and hunt me down. My best bet is to get as far away as I can and hope the dinosaurs pick up on the strong tur-kuin scent trail. Because if they come for me, I'm in for a world of pain.

A shriek cries out behind me.

The hunt is resumed.

World of pain it is.

19

The pain begins long before any of the cresties have even seen me. The impact of every hurried step I take sends a jolt of pain from my chest wound. Chills begin to spread over my skin and my stomach clenches tight. The infection is still fighting for supremacy and the last thing I should be doing right now is sprinting through the jungle.

Actually, that's not quite true. The last thing I should be doing is letting myself be eaten by a dinosaur. That pretty well trumps the infection. So I fight the growing weight in my legs and push forward, to who knows where.

If the cresties had actually seen me, I'd be done. I won't be able to put up much of a fight in my condition. But they're still tracking me by scent, no doubt following the subtle odor of my infected wound. Like any predator, their preference is always the sick, wounded, young or old. The less fight, the less chance of injury.

As they track my scent, they'll stop every few steps to test the air. They know I'm sick, and that I'll eventually tire and stop. So there's no need for them to rush. They'll expend less energy and still get a meal.

But the fact that they're not hot on my heels doesn't let me slow down. If I can reach a river, or find a crack in the ground or some other kind of shelter, I might be able to escape. So I keep running, and continue growing weaker.

My foot is just inches from the ground when I suck in a quick breath and freeze. There's an odd, unnatural rise on the forest floor. I pull my foot back, carefully place it on the ground and crouch to inspect the aberration. I brush aside a few leaves and find a tripwire, but this one is made from frayed twine, not the hard line the Arab man carried.

Someone else laid this trap.

I follow the line to its end and find it tied off to a stake in the ground. I move to the other end and find the line attached to a thick vine holding back a large branch. It's a crude trap, meant to knock someone silly, or perhaps dissuade a cresty from passing. I leave the trap be and continue past, hoping that it will be discovered by one of the dinosaurs pursuing me.

When I reach the edge of the jungle ten minutes later, I'm moving slowly, using Whipsnap like a walking stick to keep myself from falling over. But when the trees clear, I find myself distracted from my condition, and from the dinosaurs tracking me down.

A giant stone wall covered with patches of purple moss cuts through the jungle. It's at least twenty-five feet tall and stretches into the jungle as far as I can see in either direction. It's clearly ancient, exposed when the ice melted. Its construction is phenomenal. The stones it's built from are gigantic; each must weigh several tons. But even more impressive is the way they're all fit perfectly together, as though the pieces were carved by lasers. It's a work of art, really, beautiful to look at, but also a reminder that Nephilim once roamed the Earth in broad daylight.

As they do once more.

Despite the wall's presence being an ominous reminder of the size of my enemies, it also presents a possible escape route. The seams are tight, and the purple moss is no doubt slippery, but I've scaled worse, and I still have my climbing claws. The only real problem is my faltering health.

Better get started, I think, and wade into the clearing of tall grass that stands between the jungle and the wall. As I leave the jungle canopy, the sun strikes me full on for the first time. I flinch in pain, placing a hand over my eyes to help block out the light. But I don't give in to the pain. I keep my squinted eyes turned up at the wall, looking for the best place to climb.

That's when I stub my toe. As I pitch forward, I put my weight on Whipsnap, hoping to keep myself upright. But the flexible staff bends under my weight and I plummet to the ground. I'm expecting a soft thump in the grass, but I strike several hard, knobby surfaces when I hit.

I lie on the hard, unwelcoming ground for a few moments and let my eyes close. Sleep nearly claims me, but a distant cresty cry snaps my eyes back open. I push myself up and a horrible surprise greets me. The fleshless face of a Nephilim stares back at me. Startled, I scramble away from the bones, but I stop once the rest of the grisly scene comes into view.

It's a Nephilim skeleton, short by warrior standards, but far taller than the tallest human being. But what's most interesting about the skeleton is that it is entwined with a crestie skeleton. They died here together, locked in battle. The cresty's jaws are wrapped around the Nephilim's head, its long canine sticks through a clean hole in the Nephilim's skull. The weak spot. Whether the long dead dinosaur knew to bite the giant there or just got lucky is impossible to tell. But the effect was clear. The cresty killed this Nephilim, and by the positioning of the giant's hand, it looks like he managed to strike a killing blow as well, though the weapon, whatever is was, is now missing.

Taken, I realize when I see that the warrior's hand has been pried open. Someone has been here. Most likely the same some-one who set that trap. But who? I look at the excavated bodies again. They've been exhumed with care. *This is a dig site!* Some archeologist has been here. I'm sure of it.

My excitement is short-lived. A loud shifting sound slides out of the jungle. I recognize it immediately. The cresties who hunted in the cavern that I called home for several years used this technique. They would rub their bodies against the subter-ranean trees, coating them with fresh scent. They would then position themselves so that their prey fled into the trees, and when the prey smelled the fresh scent, they'd panic, stop and be caught from behind. It was a clever tactic, but it didn't work on hunters. It seems that these cresties, like the turkuins, have yet to figure out that I am a hunter. Which is fine by me. Let them rub up against the trees and set a trap. I'll be gone by the time they're done.

I'm about to get out my climbing claws, when I see a snake at my feet and jump back. My heart pounds hard in my chest and chills sweep over my skin. But my fear is misplaced. It's not a snake at all.

It's a rope.

I pick up the line and bundle it quickly. It's about forty feet long and one end is frayed, like it was hacked apart from some missing end. I don't put in much thought as to why the rope is there, or who left it. I just quickly tie one end off to Whipsnap, and with a heave, throw the weapon up and over the top of the wall. I pull the line down slowly until Whipsnap snags on something.

The shuffling sound gets louder. The cresties are closing in. With no time to test my weight on the line, I grab hold and start pulling myself up. I've only gone five feet when my arms start shaking. After another five feet, I'm sure I'm going to fall. I loop the rope around my foot and let it take my weight. I catch my breath for a moment, but then my time runs out.

With a shriek, the first of the cresties catches sight of me, and charges. The dinosaur is like a cross between a raptor and a T-rex. They've got large, sharp talons and powerful jaws, and a distinctive crest over their heads—hence the cresty name. The thing is a blur of green and red as it charges toward the wall. It's not a large specimen, just twelve feet from snout to tail. But it's big enough, and strong enough, to leap up and yank me down. As the beast prepares to do just that, I reach up with my hands, grab tight and yank myself up. I move fast and manage to pull my feet up, too.

The cresty jumps and misses my toes by inches. Fueled by a surge of adrenaline, I complete my climb in seconds. The cresty roars in frustration. I quickly pull the rope up, and then retrieve Whipsnap from the other side of the wall where it caught on a nearby tree branch. More cresties arrive, screeching up at me. I lean over the side to look at them and I'm overcome with nausea. I nearly fall into their waiting jaws, but I collapse on top of the wall instead.

I breathe hard, pulling air in through my nose. Several new scents strike me at once. The pungent smell of the dinosaurs comes first, but there's something else. Something familiar. Metallic. Gun powder? I'm not sure if that's the actual scent, but I smelled the same thing when the Arab man fired his gun. Whoever was here fired a weapon.

From the *top* of the wall.

I look at the rope piled next to me and find *two* frayed ends instead of just the one. I take hold of one end and pull it free. It's the same rope, but only teen feet long. I have just used the same escape route of the person who was here before. Except that they shot the rope to sever it. Had the cresties tried to climb the rope? It doesn't seem possible, but they are fairly smart. If I hadn't pulled the rope up so quickly, they might have tried the same with me.

As the adrenaline wears off, exhaustion returns in spades. I can feel myself crashing. I'm safe from the cresties up here, but I'm fully exposed to the sun. My fair complexion earned me a couple of nasty sunburns as a child, but I've been underground so long that I think things will be far worse now. My skin is pasty-white and might burn to a crisp inside of a half hour.

At least the sun doesn't feel warm. The storm must have brought in cool air, because unlike before, the air is now a nice seventy-something degrees. Of course, that doesn't affect how quickly your skin reacts to the ultraviolet wavelength. It could be freezing out and I'd still burn.

Sunburn or not, I'm done. As I slide down and lay on my stomach, I turn my head to the side. There, on the wall next to me, is something strange. It's blue. And square. I reach out for it and feel soft fabric. Manmade fabric of the 100% cotton variety. I grasp the cloth and pull it to my face. Up close, I can see it's a bandana.

My hand trembles as I place the fabric against my nose and breathe deep. A mix of scents triggers memories.

The strongest scent is a dog. Not any dog I know, but canines have a distinct odor. Whoever this bandana belongs to is a dog owner.

I smell dirt, sweat and an amalgam of other odors, but only one more jumps out at me. When I separate the smell from the rest, I'm overcome with something close to desperation mixed with elation. If I weren't just moments from delirium I would shout out, hoping the owner of this bandana was still nearby.

I know who owns this bandana.

The dig site, its location on the continent and the scent of Old Spice permanently bonded to the fabric leaves no doubt in my mind.

Dr. Clark has been here.

Merrill.

My friend, Aimee's husband, Mira's father, has returned to Antarktos.

I try to push myself up. Look for other clues. But the world is spinning now. The fever has returned in force.

"Merrill," I mumble.

The words of my dream return to me. "I'm here," I say. "I'm right here."

20

Memories mix with dreams. I vaguely remember standing up on the wall. The ocean lay in one direction and the endless stretch of gray wall, about eight feet across, led inland—the direction I picked. I stumbled along the top of the wall, nearly falling over the edge on more than one occasion. I kept my gaze turned down from the sun, but even with the sunglasses on, the reflected light on the stones stung my eyes.

I have vague memories of strange sounds, distant and close. Popping like fireworks. Snapping tree limbs. The wind shifting through leaves. Screams. The sounds, perhaps distorted by my fever, sounded like ghosts haunting the endless jungle that hugged the wall on either side. Eventually, perhaps hours after beginning my delirious hike, the jungle began to encroach on the wall.

It has now entirely overtaken the structure. Tree limbs stretch over the wall from either side. Up ahead I can see where the jungle canopy envelopes the wall like it's a subway car moving underground. While it will be nice to be back in the shade, the limbs make moving more difficult as I have to climb over them. This might not normally pose a challenge, but in my current state, I find walking on even ground to be difficult, never mind an obstacle course.

I stumble and catch myself on a branch. I close my eyes for a moment, and when I open them again, the jungle is moving around me, spinning in slow circles. But within that spin, I see something wonderful.

A centipede. The foot long creature clings to a branch just a few feet ahead. Its head is twisted in my direction, its antennae twitching, and like all the other creatures from the underworld, it doesn't flee from me, as it should. It looks identical to the underground variety of centipede, though there is a little bit of red in its shell now. Still, it must be the same species. I can use its flesh to ward off this infection. And since it's not the giant-sized Behemoth-eating variety, I shouldn't have any trouble catching it, that is, if I can focus on it for more than a moment.

I reach for Whipsnap, but find the weapon already in my hand. I vaguely remember using it as a walking stick. I would normally skewer the centipede through the head, ending its life quickly, but I can't trust my aim. So I opt for a different tactic.

Moving slowly, with my eyes closed, I turn Whipsnap so the mace end is on top. I open my eyes and the world shifts from left to right. I close them again. And every time I open them, the shift begins anew. Assuming I'm seeing things right during that first fraction of a second, I open and close my eyes over and over, until I have a good sense of where the creature really is. Then I close my eyes, steady myself and strike.

The swing is fast and solid, connecting with a branch on the way down. There is a snap and then a clang as Whipsnap's metal mace strikes the stone wall. I open my eyes to look, but I'm off balance from the strike, and I spill to the side. I drop my weapon on the wall as I careen over the side of it, but my descent is arrested by two thick branches that catch me under my armpits.

As my head clears, I push myself back onto the wall and look back at the tree whose branches saved my life. "Thank you, Ent," I say with a delirious grin. If only I had an army of trees to help. Right now, all I have is a very dead, very squished, centipede. I kneel next to the shattered body, scooping its small amount of flesh out of its carapace and off the stone wall. When I have a handful, I rub it onto my chest wound. I can feel the rough scabbing break away as I rub the goop in, but that's good. The centiflesh needs to get into the wound.

The pain of the freshly opened wound is intense, but I finish the job, confident that the healing properties of the centipede's meat will do its work. Exhausted and doubting my ability to navigate the congested path in my current state, I find a spot shaded by some large, palm-like leaves, and lay down with a branch under my head.

Hours later, more fireworks start. They're far away, just echoes really. The finale comes with an unbelievable crescendo of pops. *Am I really hearing this?* I wonder. The sound is so out of place. I listen for more, lying with my face turned toward the shaded jungle, but hear nothing. Movement in my periphery—the sky—catches my attention. Without thinking, I look up. The bright blue sky makes me shout in pain and close my eyes. But in that brief look, I saw something.

A man.

Flying?

Not possible.

I replay the second-long image.

The man was dressed in beige, his arms and legs flailing.

Was he falling?

Couldn't be. Not straight down anyway. There's nothing to fall from. The motion was from right to left, but also downward. He was falling, but in an arc, like he was launched from a cannon.

Or thrown by something very large.

Then it hits me. The fireworks are gunshots. And if the man sailing by overhead was thrown... Modern man is meeting the Nephilim for the first time, and the results are exactly as I expected—disastrous.

I sit up, and I'm happy to find the world no longer spinning. I'm still feeling tired, and my chest is burning, but I recognize the healing pain as different from that of the infection. Thanks to the centipede's sacrifice, I'll be back to full health within a day. For now, I'm tired and slow, and I won't be much good in a fight, but I need to find out who that man was. Based on his speed and direction, I'm pretty sure I can figure out where he landed.

Instead of scaling down the wall, I find a tree full of twisting branches and easily make my way down. Using the wall as a guideline, I turn in the direction the man flew, and begin my search.

The job is easier than I thought it would be. My health is returning, the ground beneath my feet is even for the most part and nothing tries to eat me. A hole in the canopy reveals where the man's body re-entered the jungle. His body lies in a twisted heap, thirty feet beyond. His limbs are all broken, as are, I suspect, his spine and nearly every other bone in his body. But somehow, his face escaped without much more than a few scrapes.

Crouching next to him, I look at his closed eyes. He has Asian features, but I'm not sure what country he's from until I see the red flag. Chinese. The man's uniform looks like any average soldier's, designed for trekking through the jungle, but the single star on his shoulder identify him as a low ranking general.

What is a Chinese General doing on Antarktos?

Avoiding the blood soaked into his uniform, I search his pockets for clues. The first thing I find is his identification. It looks official, but most of it is in Chinese. The only English lettering I see is his name. I read it aloud. "Zhou Kuan-Yin. What are you doing here, General?"

His other pockets reveal nothing, but I find a package of dried meat, a lighter and a pack of cigarettes. I toss the smokes, but keep the lighter and the food. The only pocket I haven't checked is over his chest, and it's covered in blood. But the boxy lump beneath the fabric hints at something worth finding.

Using a stick, I pry the pocket open and try to see what's inside. All I can see is something shiny. Like plastic. I try to fish it out with the stick, but it's not happening. Using the stick to hold the pocket open, I reach my other hand toward the pocket. I feel like I'm playing a game of Operation, trying to remove the funny bone without hitting the metal sides and setting off an unsettling buzzer. But the buzzer here is my nerves. I have dealt with a lot of dead creatures over the past few years, and even held Riodan's dead body, but human blood is something I'm still not used to. My own, sure—there's been an abundance of it spilled—but not someone else's. No thanks. The smell alone is bad enough, but the sick angles of this man's broken limbs and the knowledge that he was killed by a Nephilim, have me unsettled enough. Getting his blood on me would just be the last straw.

I find the hard plastic object with my thumb and index finger. I pull it out slowly until my finger scrapes across something sticky wet. "Gah!" I shout. I flinch and yank my hand out, flinging the thing onto the jungle floor.

After wiping my hand off on a leaf, I find the object freed from Zhou's pocket. It's hard white plastic with a rubber-sealed seam around the middle. *Waterproof,* I think. I flip the thing over, looking for blood, and finding none, I pick it up. It fits nicely in the palm of my hand. There are four small snap locks on each side of the rectangular case. I pop the locks and slowly open it.

There's a device inside. It's rectangular and has a shiny surface. I take it out of the case and flip it over. The back is smooth and black, but there are a few buttons on the thing's shiny metal edges. I have no idea what it is, but I recognize the power symbol on one of the buttons.

I push it.

The device nearly falls from my hand as I jump in surprise when a swirling, blue logo appears on what I now know is a small screen. The color is more vivid than any TV I've ever seen and the image is far clearer.

It's been more than twenty years, I remind myself. This is the future.

I smile at my caveman response to technology for a moment, and put my encyclopedic knowledge of computers to the task of figuring this thing out. Granted, my computer was an Apple II C and took up an entire desktop, but I knew how to use it better than my parents. Unfortunately for me, the menu that pops up is labeled in Chinese, so even if there was a keyboard on this thing, I don't think typing in LIST or RUN is going to do any good. I try to look through the menu with the buttons on the side, but nothing happens. I'm about to give up on the thing when I decide to access a different knowledge-base: science fiction. This is the future after all. I've seen more than a few TV episodes and movies where computers are nothing more than hand held tablets...with touchable screens.

Could we really be that far? I wonder, and touch the screen with my finger. The icon blinks beneath my touch and a new menu opens. This one makes even less sense than the first. I click on a left facing arrow at the top of the screen, and I'm delighted by the device's intuitive design. I look at the small icons and go through the list, hoping to find something that makes sense. I strike jackpot with the fourth icon.

It's a map, or at least I think it is. It's hard to tell, and there's a blinking green dot at the center. "What is this?" I say to Zhou's still, bent form.

Touching the screen, I'm able to slide the map back and forth, and up and down, but the green dot stays rooted in place. As I'm trying to figure out exactly what this is a map of, my thumb taps the screen. In the moment that both fingers touch the screen, the map image shrinks, revealing more terrain.

"Whoa!" I smile, glance up at Zhou and stop. It doesn't feel right to smile next to the dead man's body. So I collect the case and the food, and head back toward the wall, fiddling with the device as I walk. Repeating the motion with my thumb and index finger, I shrink the map repeatedly until I recognize it for what it is—Antarctica. And just like the Arab's paper map, this one has a red dot blinking right at the South Pole.

Why is everyone trying to get to the South Pole? It's not even the South Pole anymore.

If the red dot signifies the goal, what is the green dot? I wonder. By pinching my fingers together, I'm able to zoom back in on the green dot. As I'm walking and wondering, something happens. The green dot bounces ahead.

Why is the green dot moving?

My smile returns as I realize what it is and say, "No…" in disbelief.

I walk forward. Nothing happens.

So I run.

Fifty feet into my run, the green dot shifts again.

The green dot is me! Or, at least, this device. Not only is this a map, but it's some kind of tracking device so you can see where you are and where you need to go. Ingenious! I continue forward, watching the green dot shift with me. I slow as inspiration strikes. I zoom out again, and shift the map to the left, and then to the right. And I see what I'm looking for.

A winding river that leads to a lake.

Like the one from my dream.

"I'm here," the person said. "I'm right here."

I begin my sprint anew, now knowing that it will eventually lead me to a river, and then the lake. "I'm coming," I say.

21

The smell of blood hits me so strongly that I realize I've been so enraptured with watching my progress on the map that I missed the first hints of it on the breeze. Or perhaps I was just upwind of it? Doesn't matter. Because I'm surrounded by the stench now.

I stop in my tracks and slowly pocket the *maptrack*—that's what I've decided to call it. Not exactly creative, but it has a ring. With the device put away, I focus on my surroundings. The scent of blood is everywhere, which is probably because there are bodies everywhere. Hundreds of men lay scattered over the jungle floor, some crushed, some skewered on tree limbs and some in pieces. The savagery of the attacks reveals the enemy they faced to be Nephilim. The number of weapons I see laying about, along with thousands of scattered shell casings, means that these men were the source of what I mistook for fireworks. The amount of bullets zinging through the air must have been copious. Not even the cresties could stand against such power. But the Nephilim…they wouldn't have any trouble. In fact,

JEREMY ROBINSON   149

they would likely take pleasure in the pain.

The uniforms on the dead men match Zhou's, so I know they're Chinese. This must be where he was thrown from. I stand in silence for several minutes, just listening. I don't hear anything except a faint rustling in the leaves. The Nephilim that did this have left. And every other living thing in the jungle is avoiding the area. Normally, the smell of death would attract scavengers like turkuins, but there's another scent in the air keeping them at bay.

Nephilim blood.

A lot of it.

With Whipsnap in my hand, I walk into the field of dead. I try to keep my eyes off the slain men. Most of them are young, not much older than me. And their deaths were gruesome, to say the least. Dark spots of earth, damp with blood, act as a maze. I wind my way through the field of dead until I see it.

A Nephilim body.

I work my way toward the body and discover a purple pool of blood where the thing's head should be. I search the area and find bits of Nephilim flesh clinging to tree trunks. My eyes widen with the realization that some kind of explosive took the monster's head clean off. Yet another way to kill them: if you can't reach the weak spot or drown them, blow their head to bits, weak spot and all.

That it took nearly two hundred men to kill one Nephilim isn't very encouraging, though. And it was probably a lucky shot. But maybe, if men can be taught how to kill the Nephilim, they—we—might have a chance. Now if only I can find someone that isn't dead or trying to kill me. That would be a good start.

I try to identify the Nephilim, but it's hard without a head, and the armor made from feeder leather reveals nothing. What I do know is that it wasn't alone. Large Nephilim footprints are everywhere. If I had to guess, I'd say there were four of them.

If the Nephilim know people are on Antarktos, and are out looking for them, I'm going to have to be more careful. No more watching myself on the maptrack. The thing must run on batteries anyway. Probably best to shut it off until I need to course correct. But I also need to do a better job of concealing myself. My pale white skin wasn't a problem underground because there was rarely a long line of sight in the tunnels. But out here, where I can see for hundreds of feet, my white skin is a beacon. Well, it's not quite anymore. I look down at my body. I wouldn't say I'm tan, but I'm no longer quasi-translucent, either. Nor am I sunburned, which is odd, but not something I'm going to complain about.

It takes ten minutes, but I find a dead soldier who is in one piece and remove his backpack. Most of the items inside are crushed and ruined, but there is more dried food—fruit this time—and an olive green poncho. Perfect. I take the poncho and throw it over my head. The plastic texture feels funny on my skin, and the shifting sound it makes is annoying—especially with the hood up—but the green hue now covering my body will make for nice camouflage.

As the sun finally begins to set, I make my way out of the killing field and back into the jungle. I travel for several miles, stopping only when the sun has ducked fully below the horizon. I help myself to the dried meat. It's surprisingly bland—I've had better underground—but at least it's nourishing. I follow the meat with some of the dried fruit—apples, bananas, dates and raisins. The flavor feels so intense that I start laughing. I had forgotten how delightful sugar tastes! I eat half the package and force myself to stop. This isn't the time to forget the discipline that kept me alive while living underground. That I learned how to ration my food from Ninnis is never a fond memory, but the lesson has served me well.

Some long dormant instinct tells me to sleep now that night has fallen. But I'm not really tired, and night is no longer a hindrance. The light of the moon and stars, even when filtered through the canopy, is more than enough for me to see by. And with my newly acquired poncho, I'll be able to move swiftly without fear of being detected, at least not by men with guns. Nephilim and other underworld denizens will still be hunting. *All the more reason to stay awake.*

I set off at a run, occasionally checking my position on the maptrack. I angle my trajectory so that I'm closing in on the winding river, while moving up toward the lake, which, right now, is my destination.

I'm right here...

And I continue on this course for days. I occasionally come across cresty tracks and other signs of life and death, but no more people, and no Nephilim. I sleep only occasionally, during the brightest hours of the day. My eyes adjust to the sun and I can look at the sky, with my sunglasses on, without feeling pain. I suspect that in a few weeks I won't need the sunglasses at all. The infection is gone, and my wound has healed sufficiently, though the frequent opening and closing of the wound has left a scar. Justin would say it makes me look tough. And he'd be right. It does look tough.

When I finally reach the river, just miles from the lake, I shed my poncho and wade into the water. I expect it to be cold, but it feels as warm and comfortable as the jungle air. But it's no less refreshing. I drink greedily, wash days of grime and strong scent from my body and enjoy a few minutes in the direct sunlight. The sun is still uncomfortable on my eyes, but I want to condition myself. Not being able to fight in broad daylight would be a serious liability, especially now that Antarktos lies at the equator and the days are quite long.

But a few minutes is all I can take. I gather my poncho and return to the shade of the jungle. I follow the river inland and soon make it to the lake. It's a massive expanse of water, reflecting the blue sky. Beyond the river, I see the beginnings of a mountain range. It's a picturesque place, and it would be peaceful, if not for the knowledge that killers lurk nearby. In my dream, the figure I saw stood on a small beach on the right side of the lake. I can't see that far from here, but I know where I need to go.

I slip up to the edge of the jungle and watch the river and lake. When I'm certain no one is around, I dive into the water and swim quickly across. Back in the jungle, I follow the curve of the lake, moving quickly but a little more cautiously. The lake, like the river, would be a gathering place for predator and prey in search of water. So I move slowly and do my best to spot signs of habitation. After crossing two game trails covered in tracks that I recognize as belonging to the oversized albino goats I shared a cavern with underground, I come across a muddy beach where the trees and brush along the shoreline thin.

After pulling the poncho's hood up over my head, I inch closer to the muddy clearing. There are footprints—boot prints actually. And a few different sizes. Some are clearly men, larger and deeper from weight, but one set is smaller, either a woman's or a small man's. What were they doing here? Getting a drink? Following the lake like I am? Will I run into them?

I step closer, careful not to leave any prints of my own. That's when I see an entirely different kind of indentation. A dog! A large dog, but still, a dog!

I take out the blue bandana and smell it. After getting the dog's scent in my nose, I take it away and smell the air.

Nothing. It's been a little while since they were here. No scents linger. But still, what are the odds that someone else brought a dog to Antarktos? As I crouch atop a rock, looking at the boot prints, I notice a tiny detail. A hair. It's just one, partly squished into the mud by a boot, but it's blond and sticks out. I pull the strand free and fight my rising emotions. The hair is blond, coarse and tightly bent at odd angles.

I have seen this hair before.

I have felt it against my face and neck.

This is Mira's hair!

I'm sure of it.

I stand up, fully prepared to shout her name like an idiot. But I never get the chance. I'm struck from behind. Not by a weapon, fist or anything physical, but by a smell. The wind has shifted direction. And it carries the scent of a human being masked by mud, dung and blood.

There is a hunter behind me.

22

The attack comes fast as the hunter notices the shift in the wind. A faint shift is all I hear, but I know my enemy is airborne. I leap in the only direction available to me, spinning with Whipsnap at the ready. I land in knee-deep water, which I strike with Whipsnap, sending a distracting splash toward the hunter.

As I charge out of the water, I get my first look at my adversary. It's a man. Perhaps twice my age, with far bigger muscles than me. He's also completely bald, which is something I have yet to see in a hunter, but why not? Baldness is caused by an excess of testosterone, and from what I can see, this man has testosterone to spare. His clothing does nothing to reveal which Nephilim he serves, but his weapon, a razor sharp scimitar, hints at one of the ancient Persian gods.

My sudden reversal seems to startle the hunter. He didn't know who I was, I realize. The hooded poncho not only conceals my identity, but he likely also mistook me for a modern soldier. I use his confusion to my advantage, striking his sword to the side.

With the man off balance, I spin and let Whipsnap spring out, sweeping the man's legs out from under him. He lands in the mud with a wet slap that knocks the air out of his lungs.

The hunter is now at my mercy, but what should I do? I will not kill him. It's not even a consideration. But I can't just let him go. I'll have to knock him unconscious and make my escape. He doesn't know who I am, so the Nephilim won't be alerted to my presence.

To my surprise, the hunter drops his weapon and asks, "Who are you?"

It's a question I won't answer. I don't even want him to hear my voice. The less he knows, the better. I step closer and raise a fist to knock the man silly.

"Wait," he says, and I nearly do. But exposure is something I can't risk. As my fist comes down, my arm is yanked back by a sudden weight. I stumble away from the man and find my arm wrapped in strong cords attached to three heavy metal balls. The weapons are called bolas and while their intended used was to trip up fleeing livestock, they work just as well on people.

The second hunter explodes from the forest and lands next to the fallen man. He is short, but has taut, sinewy muscles. Where the first man is strong, this man is quick. His dark skin and flat nose have the distinct look of an Australian aborigine. His dark red dreadlocks are pulled back in a thick ponytail. With his eyes locked on me, he extends a hand to the bald man and pulls him up.

What the...? Hunters do *not* help each other. Are these men friends? Have they been ordered to keep each other from harm?

"Careful of this one," the big hunter says while retrieving his sword. "He's one of us."

"Show us your face," the aborigine hunter says.

In response, I begin twirling Whipsnap in my hands, letting my actions speak louder than words. If they think they're going to get anything out of me, they're going to have to beat it out of me.

A few things about my actions strike me. I'm being bold in the face of severe danger, like Ull, but it feels natural now—a part of me. Not only that, I'm fully confident in my abilities. These hunters are no doubt skilled, but I am Solomon Ull Vincent, the Last Hunter, who was not only trained by Ninnis—the most skilled hunter—but also defeated Ninnis in combat. I can handle these two.

The realization makes me smile.

And when the two hunters see my grin, they look a little less sure of themselves.

The aborigine tilts his head up and lets out a loud, bird-like call.

What is he doing?

Voices rise up in the distance. A lot of them.

He called for help.

This is also decidedly non-hunter behavior, but before I can think things through, the two men press the attack. Intimidated by my behavior or not, they're still hunters, and they won't back down—especially with help on the way.

The bald man approaches and swings his sword wildly. It's a messy attack, but the random strikes are hard to block. I step back, waiting for an opening and just as I'm about to strike, my legs are suddenly bound, wrapped tight with more bolas. The moment I'm immobilized, the bald hunter's attack becomes focused and skilled.

I hop back with my feet bound and block three strikes, the third coming very close to my face. With another big leap, I place Whipsnap's sharp blade between my bound ankles and slice through the lines. My legs are free by the time I land. The bald man barely has time to register that my feet are free, when I kick up hard and catch him under the jaw. His head snaps back and he falls over, unconscious.

I hear the whoosh of another set of bolas whipping toward me, and I duck. But as my body moves down, I thrust Whipsnap up, catch the bolas and use their spinning momentum to redirect their course. I fling the bolas back as the hunter lunges toward me. One of the stones strikes his head, and he falls to the ground beside his bald partner.

As I believed, the pair is no match for me. But, they are not alone. Hunters emerge from the jungle like angry fire ants on the prowl. They see their fallen comrades, and me standing above them, and the attacks come hard and fast.

I have no time to look carefully at who I'm fighting. There is only time to react. I dive into the jungle as an arrow twangs into a tree trunk beside my head. The thick brush surrounding the lake clears, as I move away from the water. When a knife thunks into a tree I just passed, it becomes clear that I will not be able to outrun this group of hunters. So I need to stand and fight, and hopefully do enough damage to make them think twice about continuing their pursuit. It's unlikely, but it's my only option, because if I keep running, one of these arrows or knives is going to bury itself into my back.

I enter a ten-foot clearing surrounded by tall tree trunks. It will give me room to maneuver, but not so much that they can attack me all at once. I skid to a stop, spin around and am greeted by an airborne hunter with an axe raised above his head.

I dive and roll to the side as the man sails past. When he lands, I kick him square in the back. The kick, added to his momentum, sends him sprawling forward and he slams into a tree.

An arrow passes through my poncho between my arm and my rib cage.

Too close!

Two more hunters enter the clearing. I can see at least ten more coming, including the recovered aborigine and the bald hunter.

This is a fight I cannot win.

But I have no choice.

I block a sword strike to my right, and kick out a knee to the left. With a spin, I disarm the swordsman, but I'm sucker-punched by a female hunter who snuck up behind me. A blind kick catches her in the stomach, and I hear her drop. I turn the mace end of Whipsnap on the disarmed swordsman and shove. He shouts in pain as the spikes pierce his skin. It won't be a mortal wound, but it hurts. The blow staggers the man back.

A knife strikes my left arm, but it's a superficial wound. The baggy poncho is hiding my body and making it hard to target my limbs. But why are they targeting my limbs and not my core?

And why did the woman behind me punch instead of stab or bludgeon me? Here we are, a bunch of hunters, and no one is trying to kill anyone?

Something is definitely screwy with this situation.

Five hunters leap into the clearing. I spin Whipsnap's bladed edge around in a wide circle, forcing the group to leap back. But their appearance was a distraction. I'm struck from behind again, this time with something much larger than a fist. The broad, stone weapon feels like the top of a very large hammer. The impact sends me flying and knocks the air from my lungs. But I've been trained to ignore pain and fight without breathing, so I turn my fall into a roll and turn to face my attacker.

There are not one, but two women. One holds a hammer, the other—who I assume is the one I kicked—holds two throwing knives. They're backlit by a beam of sunlight that stings my eyes, but there's something familiar about them.

"Look at his weapon," the hammer-wielding woman says.

The shorter of the two women—the one with the knives—stiffens and with an angry voice, shouts, "Where did you get that?"

Shoot. I hadn't even considered that Whipsnap's unique design would be recognizable to hunters.

A knife flies through the air, just missing my arm as I spin. A second one follows, cutting through my poncho's arm on the other side. I'm forced back by the barrage of knives, which are thrown with a skill I have only seen once before.

I know who this is.

I know who the woman with the hammer is!

But I'm unable to speak their names as the air has yet to return to my lungs.

The knife-wielding woman is in a rage. She's going to kill me without realizing who I am!

I stagger back against a tree. The woman steps out from the light and I see her face for the first time in months. It's so wonderful that I nearly miss her eyes locking on my forehead. Her hand pulls back and snaps forward, releasing a knife.

In one fluid motion, I toss Whipsnap up, and duck my head down. The knife passes between the top of my head and the hood. With the poncho pinned to the tree by the knife, I duck down out of it, shedding it like a skin, and emerge in time to catch Whipsnap. But I'm too late.

There's a hammer raised to strike. Two knives raised to throw. An assortment of other weapons, too, held by at least fifteen more hunters.

But they're all frozen in place as though my eyes belonged to the gorgon, Medusa.

I try to catch my breath and speak, but all I manage is a wheeze.

It doesn't matter, though. I hear a telltale gasp and the two knives drop to the ground.

"Solomon?" Em says. "Is it really you?"

I smile and nod, dropping Whipsnap to the ground. Em rushes to me. She's got all of her blades, around her waist and chest, looking as dangerous as ever, except for the pixie-like hairdo that's a result of her shaving her head when she pretended to be my wife. She leaps into my arms. I squeeze her tight, enjoying the sensation of feeling loved for the first time in a long time. Hunters never cry. I'm usually the only exception. But I'm not alone today. Em squeezes me hard and lets out a joyful sob.

I hear whispers all around me as the strange turn of events is explained. I hear only bits and pieces. "Solomon." "The Last Hunter." "Tartarus." "His hair."

Weapons lower.

Tension melts.

And then the strangest thing I think I've seen since arriving on this continent takes place. This squad of deadly hunters drops to one knee and bows their heads.

To me.

23

"We thought you were dead. Gone forever," Em says, still clinging to me and oblivious to the bowing hunters around us.

"I came back," I say, stating the obvious.

"How did you escape Tartarus?" The voice is unbelieving, yet surprised.

I look up and see Kainda's strong body step out of the light. Unlike the others, she's not bowing. Her skin is deeply tanned, and she's dressed in black leathers. There isn't even a hint of a smile on her face, but she's a vision. Em has always been a sister to me. Kainda is...something else. I'm not sure. As Ninnis's daughter, she was offered to me as a wife, which I—being the impetuous Ull at the time—rudely turned down. Insulted, Kainda became a bitter rival out for blood. But when we met next, I saved her life, and when Ull's personality emerged, I felt something for her. And now, that personality is part of the whole person I have become. My first impression of Kainda was that she was much older than me, but time is funny in the underworld and she now looks about my age. But I also think it has something to do with her current lack of makeup. I hadn't realized she'd been decorating her face before, but her natural beauty is now clear to see. As is her confusion, from my lingering stare.

"I left," I say.

"You just left?" Kainda sounds annoyed by my answer. "You were in *Tartarus*."

I understand her confusion. Tartarus is a place regarded as a tomb of eternal torture that the Nephilim fear more than anything else. When I stepped through that door, I had no idea how easy it would be to return. Not that letting go of my burden was easy. People seem to be wired to cling to the things that make them feel bad about themselves.

"It's a long story," I say, "but yes. I opened the door and walked out."

Kainda looks enraged by my casual reply. She takes her hammer and slams it into a tree. With a crack, the tree topples and nearly crushes some of the bowed hunters, but the branches tangle in the canopy and the tree's fall is arrested. "Then what the hell took you so long!?"

With that, Kainda stomps off into the jungle.

I look down at Em and ask, "Did I do something wrong?"

Em smiles up at me. "You did something right. She just wasn't expecting it."

The hunters around us stand up as Em explains.

"I knew you would come back." She motions to the others. "And they believed it too."

"We all saw what happened at the gates," the aborigine says.

"Behemoth. The fire. Nephil."

The big bald man steps forward. "When you rejected Nephil and gave up his body, some of us were…inspired by your strength. We fled to the surface, and over time have managed to find each other and band together."

A group of rogue hunters. The thought brings a smile to my face. "How many?"

"Thirty-one," Em says.

"Your army," the aborigine says.

"My *army*?"

"We have been waiting for you to return," Em says. "Preparing
for it."

"How could you have known?" I ask. While I'm thankful for their faith in my abilities, I didn't even think it was possible, so how could Em, not to mention these hunters I've never met, be so sure that I would escape Tartarus?

"Luca," Em says. "When you left, he fell into a deep sleep. He would eat, and drink on occasion, but mostly he just slept. And spoke. About you. Little of what he said made sense, but the things he described are like nothing in the underworld. When he mentioned your name, I felt sure he was seeing you, as he did before."

"You knew about the drawings?" I ask.

"I heard him tell you about them," she says. "Thin walls." Em starts collecting her knives from the trees and the ground around us. "About a week ago, Luca woke up."

"When I left Tartarus," I say.

"Said he saw you in his dreams," Em says. "Said you were flying over the lake. Tried to call you."

"I'm here," I say. "I'm right here."

"What?" she says.

"I saw him on the shore, yelling to me. It's what led me here."

She stops, looks at me and smiles. "Tobias would be proud of you."

I look around at the group of hunters. "Of both of us."

She shrugs and sheaths the last of her collected knives. Then she walks right up to me and stops. She's looking me over like an art student observing a classic painting. In that quiet moment, I return her look, remembering the face of the one I call sister. Her deep blue eyes shift back and forth, from my face to my hair. Her skin is darker, but so are the freckles on her cheeks. Her hair is still a mix of brown—her natural color—and blood red, revealing the taint of Nephilim corruption.

"How did you do it?" she asks, her voice a whisper.

"I told you," I say. "I walked out." Thinking she wants a longer explanation I add, "We all carry burdens—the weight of the bad things we've done—and in Tartarus, those—"

"What?" she says. "No. Not that. Your hair."

My hair? I haven't given my hair a second thought. A streak of blond hair emerged when I remembered who I was and fled from the Nephilim, years ago. I'd hoped more of it turned blond since, but never thought to check, not to mention I didn't have a mirror handy. The shock of hair that occasionally hangs in my face has been blond for a long time, so I haven't noticed any change. But it sounds like the red might have retreated a little more. "Has more of the red gone away?"

Em laughs and shakes her head. "Solomon…" She reaches a hand out to the bald hunter. "Krane. Your sword."

The bald man, whose name is Krane, steps forward and hands his scimitar to Em. The curved blade is wide toward the end, and very shiny. I imagine that Krane uses its reflective surface to blind opponents before striking, but it also makes for a handy mirror. She holds the flat surface of the sword up in front of me.

The face of a stranger stares back.

No…not a stranger. Someone long forgotten, mixed with an aged exterior. While I still look young, the stubble on my face has become a full-fledged beard. When I look at my bright blue eyes, I see Luca's, too, and the small razor-clawed thinker double, but mostly I see the eyes that looked back at me in my parents' bathroom mirror.

But there is something else. Something that is both new and old. And as I realize that what I'm seeing is not an illusion, my knees start to grow weak. I take the sword in my hands and fall to my knees. Turning my head in either direction, I inspect the change for any trace of corruption.

I find nothing.

My hair—every single strand—is blond.

My widening smile turns into a laugh. Now I understand, in part, why the hunters here are bowing to me. They know who I am, who I was and what I did. They know I entered Tartarus, where I stayed for three months, and I've not only returned, but I've returned purified. Free of the Nephilim corruption.

I look at each and every one of the hunters around me and see blood red hair on all except for the bald Krane. While all of them also have streaks of their original hair color to varying degrees, the red is a constant reminder of who they served, what was done to them and what they have done to others.

"You didn't know?" Em asks.

I shake my head. "There's a mirror shortage in Tartarus."

Em laughs and takes Krane's sword from me. After handing it back to the big man, she pulls me up. "We need to move."

The serious tone of her voice cuts through my relief. "What's been happening?" I ask.

"The jungle is a dangerous place. Outsiders have come. Their weapons are…"

"We lost a few hunters," Krane says.

I nearly scoff at the idea, but remember the Arab man's reaction to seeing me. And the Chinese soldiers were armed for war. But if they're shooting at people and are clearly not prepared to fight Nephilim, then who are they looking to fight?

Each other, I realize. *They're here to kill each other.*

Feeling discouraged by this revelation, I look up and find the eyes of twenty hunters on me. Are they looking for guidance? Leadership? I meet the aborigine's eyes. He seems to understand my plight and gives me a slight nod of encouragement. They're looking for hope.

I'm not ready for this, I think. I can't lead these people. They're all older, and… I nearly say they're smarter than me, but my intellect revolts. They're not smarter than me. Few people are. And they're not stronger than me, either. Even without my powers, the group had trouble fighting me, not to mention the fact that I've killed a Nephilim warrior and survived Tartarus. Maybe I am the best person for the job, but I still don't feel ready. I'd rather be home, lying in bed and staring at a map of Antarctica, the place where I was born but never meant to go.

But I'm here. And they're watching me. So I do my best to look strong and fearless and say, "Take me to…"

I falter. Take me where? To your leader? Home? Your base? Where the heck do they live anyway?

Then I realize what I really want to say. "Take me to Luca."

24

We make our way around the lake like a military platoon, quietly stalking, wary of enemies. Kainda takes the point position, scouting ahead and then giving the all clear. A small group brings up the rear, erasing our trail. I'm essentially in the middle of the group, protected like I'm the President of the United States and the hunters are my secret service. The attention makes me uncomfortable, and I don't need protecting, but there was no stopping them.

Em is near the front, too, though I can tell she doesn't want to be by the way she keeps looking back at me. We have a lot of catching up to do, not to mention strategizing, but I get the impression that she, and Kainda, despite being two of the younger hunters in this group, are in charge. Em gives orders with the calm of someone who has done so for a while, and her words are followed without question.

Her new authority feels strange to watch. When we last saw each other, we were both outcasts. Alone. And now, here she is surrounded by an army of hunters.

My army of hunters, they say.

But since no one is asking me what to do, they are still, quite clearly, Em's army. And I think I like it that way. I've caused a lot of damage and ruined a lot of lives on my own. I don't want to consider the cost if all these hunters tag along with me. I'm not saying I won't need their help. I'll need it, there's no doubt. But I will not put them in danger until I'm sure it will matter, until the benefits outweigh the risks.

"Are you okay?"

I turn to the voice and find the aborigine walking next to me. He is a skilled hunter. I didn't hear him coming, probably because I was lost in thought. "Yeah. Fine," I say.

"You seem…distracted," he says. When I don't reply, he continues. "I don't blame you. You've been through a lot."

I almost say, "You have no idea," but stop, first because it's rude, and second because I don't know who this man is, or what he's been through. Thankful for the distraction, I offer him my hand. "I'm Solomon."

He shakes it and with a grin, says, "I know."

The man's smile creases deep crow's feet on the sides of his eyes, and I wonder how he could have ever been a hunter. He's kind, soft-spoken and his eyes lack any trace of the ferocity that hunters, rehabilitated or not, cannot hide. I stop in my tracks. "You're not a hunter."

His smile is wide and full of gleaming white teeth. He reaches up and pulls the wig of red dreadlocks from his head. The hair underneath is short and black—not corrupted. "You're smart *and* a skilled fighter."

"And you're a teacher," I say.

"Have you met many other teachers?" the man asks eagerly. I suspect he hasn't met any, but would like to, perhaps to share, and work through, their tribulations.

"Just one," I say. "Aimee. She serves under the Norse." It strikes me that Aimee would have a place among these hunters. "She was my friend."

"A hunter and teacher...friends? Before this, before we escaped, most of these hunters might have beaten me for looking at them the wrong way."

He's telling the truth. Though he lives among the hunters now, and is quite skilled himself, he still fears them.

"We were friends before I was taken," I say.

"Strange that she would end up here, too," he says.

"She's here because of me." I start walking again, eyes to the ground. "She was my final test. I took her."

"Oh," he says, tagging along.

And I'm going to get her back, I determine. Even if I have to put my quest for the Jericho Shofar on hold for a day. I can't let Aimee stay with the Nephilim any longer. Not when there is someplace else for her to be.

"If she's with the Norse, she might not be too far away," he says.

I stop again. "What? Why?"

"The strongest of the warrior tribes are gathering at Olympus."

"Olympus?"

"You saw the mountain range beyond the lake?" he asks.

In my dreams and in reality, I think, but I answer only, "Yes."

"The tallest mountain, straight out from the lake, is Mount Olympus."

Not only am I close to my goal of finding Hades, who must be at Olympus, but Aimee could also be nearby. Perhaps I can visit with Hades and escape with Aimee all at once?

"I am Adoni," he says. "I have been a teacher to the aboriginal gods of Australia for nearly fifty surface years, though it felt more like ten to me. My children are now adults. My wife might be dead."

When I don't reply, he sees the sadness creeping into my face. "You have experienced the same."

"My three years have been more than twenty on the surface. I was just a boy when they took me."

"You are still just a boy," Adoni says. "The muscles and beard and status might fool most, but I can see through it."

I smile at him. Why do the Nephilim take such kind people to be their teachers? Is it because they think they're less likely to cause problems? Or try to escape? Adoni seems like he would have been capable of making a run for it. "You fight well for a teacher," I say.

"My father taught me how to hunt—animals—in the bush," Adoni says. "I suspect the Nephilim didn't know this about me when they brought me here."

"Did you ever try to escape?"

He gives a shrug. "No."

"But—"

My question is an obvious one and he answers before I can

finish. "I did more good by staying. When you've been among the Nephilim as long as I have, you are afforded a bit of freedom."

I remember finding Aimee alone in the Norse library, and nod.

"Thanks to that freedom, I was able to facilitate the escape of—"

"You helped Tobias escape with Em and Luca!"

He smiles and bows his head humbly. "Among others, some of whom are with us now. And when I heard about what you had done, I knew it was finally time for me to leave. Emilie found me not too long after that. I was sad to hear of Tobias's passing, but he managed to pass on some of his skill to Emilie, and to you."

"So you and Tobias were...friends?" I ask.

"Not at first. Like all hunters, he terrified me. And when he came to me for help, I turned him down. Twice. I thought it a ruse. A trap. It wasn't until I met young Luca that I decided to help them escape. The boy's innocence won me over. As yours does now. In fact..." He takes my arm and turns me toward him. He looks at my face, and then in my eyes. With a gasp he says, "It's true. Luca *is* a clone."

"A clone?" I ask.

"A duplicate," Adoni says. "A clone is what modern humans call an organism that is a genetic copy of the original. Luca is your clone, and unlike the others, like Xin, he is a perfect clone."

"People can do this?" I ask, feeling unsettled that the human race is working on something that feels decidedly Nephilim.

"According to my studies, it is possible. The first cloned

animal was a sheep. They've done other animals now. Pets even. Cloning people is illegal, but that doesn't mean it hasn't happened." He sees that this bothers me. "People are still people," he says. "The world hasn't changed that much in twenty years."

He might be right. People have always pushed science to questionable limits. But I don't think many people would like the idea of cloning after nearly being gutted by a half-thinker version of themselves with razor blades for fingers. Not that all of my clones are bad. "You mentioned Xin. Is he alive? Is he here?"

"Alive, yes," Adoni says. "Here, no. Despite Luca's insistence that Xin be trusted, the hunters, Kainda included, couldn't be convinced. Only Emilie and I believed the young man. That may change now that you are here."

"I'm not sure how much will change," I say.

"Now that you're here," Adoni says. "Everything will change."

Before I can reply, a voice calls out. "Solomon!"

For the first time since my conversation with Adoni began, I take a long look at my surroundings. We've entered a clearing in the trees that is still somehow covered by the thick canopy. I can see the blue glint of the lake off to my left. And to my right is the entrance to a cave. A water source, cover, quick access to the underground. Motion above pulls my eyes up, and I get my first real look at where the hunters are living—tree houses. They're crude structures built from branches and large leaves, but they're hard to see. Ropes connect the trees and can be drawn up or thrown down for access to the ground.

"Solomon!" A small body swings around a tree, leaps to the ground and rolls before running straight toward me. I recognize the nearly white hair and bright blue eyes immediately.

"Luca!" I shout.

As Luca passes Em, she crosses her arms with a smile on her face and watches her adopted brothers reunite. Krane stands just beyond her, watching the scene with curiosity. Luca leaps up with surprising skill and I catch him in the air. We squeeze each other hard and fast.

When Luca pulls back, he says, "You heard me?"

"I did," I say. "Thank you."

Luca looks around like he's making sure no one is listening, then he whispers in my ear. "Xin says hello, and don't trust anyone."

25

Don't trust anyone? *Don't trust anyone*! I would love to ask for a little clarification about what Luca has just told me, but some of the others are closing in to greet me now. Luca hops out of my arms like everything is peachy. He's still all smiles and thrilled to see me, but he gives me a quick, serious glance that says he's not joking.

Don't trust anyone…

Certainly, that doesn't include Luca.

Or Em.

But why doesn't Em know? If she did, she would have pulled me aside and told me. Instead, she let me chat it up with Adoni. I glance back at the man I'd begun to think of as a friend and find him watching me. There's nothing inherently wrong with that. *Everyone* is watching me.

Thank you, Xin, *for the paranoia.*

I almost expect him to answer, but his voice never enters my mind.

"So this is where we live," Em says. She stops behind Luca, wraps her arms around him and kisses his head.

There is very little Xin could say that would make me not trust Em. I'll tell her about the warning when I get a chance. See if she thinks any of these hunters could still be loyal to the Nephilim.

"It's, ahh, nice," I say, but I'm looking at the ground, lost in thought.

"Sol," Em says, drawing my eyes up to her. She points to the canopy. "Up there."

I glance up. "Right. I know. I saw. Kind of like an Ewok village."

Her scrunched nose confirms that I've made no sense. No one here has ever watched TV, let alone seen *Return of the Jedi*. "Forget it," I say.

She's trying to figure me out, but can't, so she moves on. "We sleep up there because there are a lot of predators in the jungle, and while we're not defenseless, it's nice to sleep without worrying about being eaten."

In the underground, sounds are contained and amplified. Predators, like the cresties, had a hard time sneaking up on a hunter without being detected. Out here, with the constant rustle of leaves in the wind, their movements could go unnoticed. Taking to the trees was a good idea. But it seems wholly inadequate. "Is it defensible?"

"Against hunters, yeah," Em says. "It is now. We have sentries roaming the jungle all around us. They'd be hard to get past without making any noise."

I point to the cave entrance. "And that's your escape route?"

Em nods. "Splits into a lot of branches that we've all memorized. None are big enough for a Nephilim."

"But it's not the Neph's we fear, is it?" Krane says. The man is so muscular and tough looking, I can't picture him fearing anyone other than a Nephilim.

"There are hunters looking for us," Em says. "Before the sentries, a few came close."

"They found us," Krane says, "But didn't live long enough to spread the word."

"You killed them?" I asked, a little surprised.

Em doesn't meet my eyes. She knows how I feel about killing human beings.

"There was little choice," Adoni says. "We tried to subdue the first with the hopes of freeing her. We lost two men for the effort. Some hunters just can't let go of their bonds."

I'm not sure I agree, but I understand their point of view. If they let her escape, they would all be in danger. If they captured her alive, how many more would have died? It's a moral dilemma I hope I never have to face.

"She found her freedom in death," Krane says.

It's cold and brutal, but I can't argue with the big man's logic.

A tug on my arm reminds me that Luca is still with us, listening to this conversation of killing and death. I feel like he shouldn't be hearing such things, but he has seen, and survived, far worse. These dark subjects are probably as familiar to him as Go-Bots and Snickers bars were to me.

"Come to the beach," Luca says. "I want to show you something."

I would like nothing more than to spend a few quiet minutes with Luca, but I can feel the eyes of these hunters watching me. They're clearly shocked by my presence and the fact that I'm alive, not to mention my hair, which honestly has me a little shaken.

"I'll be there in a few minutes," I tell Luca.

He frowns and looks at his feet. I crouch in front of him and take his shoulders. His eyes look up so we're face to face. It's like staring into a mirror that sees the past. "Have I ever lied to you?"

"No."

"When you were taken," I say, "I swore that I would get you back. And I did, right?"

He nods.

"And now I swear I will meet you at the beach." It's meant to be lighthearted, but the boy doesn't smile.

"Daddy died," he says, and throws himself into my arms. I hold the small child, thinking about how I would have handled the death of my father when I was six. Granted, Luca is a tougher child than I was, but we're still wired the same way. His tears trickle down my shoulder. His little body shakes in my arms. I can feel my eyes growing wet, too, but like I said, the hunters are watching. I can't show weakness. Not yet. Not until they know me and understand that, this...love, is where my strength comes from.

"I know," I say, squeezing the boy. "I'm sorry."

He pulls away and wipes his eyes, glancing around, and conscious that he too, is being watched, and judged. "You won't die, will you?"

"I have already been to Tartarus and back," I say. "I will not die."

Luca smiles.

"And I will meet you at the beach. In just a few minutes."

He nods. "Okay." And then he's off, running toward the beach. A child again. I envy him for a moment and then stand to face the hunters.

They've gathered in a circle. Some in the tree above me. Some on the ground, arms crossed. A few continue with what they were doing before I arrived—preparing food, sharpening weapons, stretching leather—but their eyes are on me more than on their tasks.

"You're right not to trust me," I say, taking several of them off guard, including Em, who nearly falls over when she whips around toward me. "I am the chosen vessel of Nephil, broken, corrupted and trained by Ninnis. I contained the body of Nephil for years, and his darkness sometimes consumed me. The spirit of Nephil entered me as well, and I spent the last three months in Tartarus, a land of torture for the corrupt. You have reason to not trust me."

Some hunters lower their hands, trying to look casual, but I know they're really just putting their hands closer to their weapons. Kainda, on the other hand, is a rock. Her arms are crossed over her chest. She stares at me with serious eyes, waiting for me to finish. Her gaze unnerves me far more than the hunters reaching for their weapons do, mostly because, for some reason, I care about what she thinks.

"You are hunters," I say. "You are cautious and slow to trust.

As you should be. These traits kept you alive in the underworld when you fought for your life every day. But, you no longer fight for *your* life. You fight for *each other's* lives, and for a world beyond, which some of you have never seen...and the rest have forgotten. It's time to start trusting, or you all will die."

Em looks uncomfortable, but doesn't stop me. She's probably wondering where I'm going with this just like the rest of them.

"And you will have to trust me. Most of you know me as Ull, the chosen vessel of Nephil, meant to rule over Nephilim and hunter alike. But that's just part of my name, part of who I am. My real name is Solomon Ull Vincent. I was taken from my parents and tortured by the hunter named Ninnis. For a time, I forgot myself. My home. My parents. My friends. I did things that crushed me with guilt.

"I can see your hair," I say. "The streaks of brown, black and yellow. I know you feel the weight, too. But you can be free of it. I once held the body of Nephil, it is true, but I cast it out. As I did with the spirit of Nephil. As I did with the guilt that consumed me before I opened the gates of Tartarus and stepped out. I was told that I would be the last hunter. That I would usher in the time when hunters were no longer needed. The Nephilim believed they would no longer need hunters after reclaiming the surface. But they were wrong."

I spin slowly, meeting the eyes of each and every hunter watching me. I have their attention. Even those that had been pretending to work have now stopped. "They won't need hunters," I say with a grin. "Because they'll all be dead."

Despite having given a rousing speech worthy of a Hollywood

football locker room scene, there's no cheering, no whoops, or clapping. Only silence. These are, after all, hunters. But then, one of them steps forward. He has wild spiky red hair with a blond streak front and center. His eyes are cold and focused. He moves like a snake, smooth but ready to strike. He's about my height, but stronger and older. This is a seasoned hunter, not accustomed to listening to the words of anyone save his master.

I glance at Em. She looks unsure and whispers, "He is Tunis. One of our best."

The man stops in front of me. I can't read his face. He could be seconds away from slitting my throat and I wouldn't know.

"What I want to know, last hunter," he says. "Is will *you* trust *us?*"

Xin said to trust no one, but I don't think that's a choice. Not really. If I don't show trust in them, how can I expect it in return?

We stare at each other for a moment. A simple "yes" will not convince him, or the others. I reach down to my belt and the man tenses. I move slowly, drawing my knife and hoping that Xin is wrong, or at least that this is one of the people I can trust. His eyes follow my hand, his muscles tense and ready to defend himself. But then I turn the knife toward myself and place the blade against my neck. He's so shocked by my actions that he doesn't resist when I take his hand and bring it up to the knife. When I let go, Tunis is holding the knife to my throat.

"You could kill me," I say. "There is nothing I, nor anyone else, could do to stop you. My life belongs to you."

Tunis's forehead scrunches up. What I am doing right now

makes no sense to the man. "You are wrong," he finally says, and I see something change in his eyes—understanding. He pulls the blade away from my neck and drops it to the ground. It lands between our feet, piercing the earth. "It is my life that belongs to you."

"As does mine," says another.

And then another.

The hunters each speak the words and bow their heads to me. This is different than what happened in the jungle. That was awe. Wonderment. At me being alive. And at my hair. This…is allegiance. The phrase is repeated around the circle, finishing with Em who speaks the words as seriously as the rest, despite not needing to.

Only one person remains silent. Kainda. As the others move in to greet me, she slips away.

26

I spend an hour with the hunters, learning their names, who their masters were, where they lived, what weapons they prefer—the kinds of things hunters talk about. As the group disperses slowly and the hunters go back to their work, Em clears her throat signaling that she would like a word with me. I nod a goodbye to the last few hunters and turn to Em.

"Well done," she says.

I shrug. "I'm not sure how much of this is me and how much is a show."

"Don't worry," she says. "I know you, remember? That was all you."

I'm not so sure, and certainly not as confident as I appeared. But I don't argue, mostly because there are other things I want to do.

And as usual, Em can read my mind nearly as well as Xin. She points to the right. "The beach is that way. Go. Spend some time together. We'll talk tonight."

Her words, "We'll talk tonight," carry weight. The reprieve with Luca will be short-lived.

"Krane. Adoni," Em says. "Keep an eye on them."

As I move to the lake, Krane and Adoni fall in line behind me, hands near their weapons. I should probably be wary, too, but as we reach the beach, Luca sees me and beams with excitement. He quickly shows me the sand castle he built, which is really more of a mud castle. I crouch next to him and start to feel like a kid again. I used to build castles just like this when my parents brought me to the beach.

"This is my house," Luca says. He begins decorating it with leaves, flower petals and blades of grass. "You can build a house next door."

Slightly embarrassed by the request, I look for Krane and Adoni. They've taken up positions twenty feet to either side of us, backs turned to us as they watch for trouble. I have a hundred questions for Luca, but decide the child has the right idea, and I dig into the mud. The earth is wet, but warm, no different from the air really.

Twenty minutes later, I've got a foot-tall tower built and glowing in the light of the now setting sun. It has finger indents for windows and a flag-like branch and leaf stabbed into the top. As I smooth out the sides of the tower, I say, "This means something," quoting *Close Encounters of the Third Kind*.

Luca laughs like he understands the joke and says, "What could a mud house mean?"

"I have no idea," I say.

"Are you done?" he asks.

As I take my mind off the task of building my tower, I realize that Luca has been done for several minutes. We built in silence, just enjoying being with each other, the ways kids do. It felt foreign and unnatural at first, but some part of me now feels rejuvenated. "Yeah, I think I'm done."

"Okay," he says, and starts to tear down his creation.

I stop him with a hand on his shoulder. "What are you doing?"

"Em says I can't leave any evidence," Luca says. "So we have to take them down and flatten out the ground."

"Huh," I say, "Makes sense. But…let's do it like this."

I do my best impression of a Godzilla roar, and stomp toward my castle.

"What are you doing?" Luca asks.

"Being Godzilla," I say. "Justin and I used to do this in the winter, in the snow when the plows made piles on the side of the road."

Again, Luca couldn't possibly understand what I've just said. He has no context for it. Godzilla, snow plows and roads are all foreign to him. But the wanton destruction of a freshly built mud castle seems to be a universal language to boys everywhere. Luca roars and joins in, crushing his castle beneath his feet.

"Is Godzilla like Behemoth?"

"Yeah," I say. "But not as scary. He's even a good guy sometimes."

Luca gives his castle one last stomp, flattening it out. "Good."

Then, in a flash, the boy's mind moves on to something else. "Oh, hey, come see this!" He dashes to the water's edge and stops when his toes get wet. He bends over and starts slapping the lake's surface with his hand.

"What are you doing?" I ask.

"Calling my friends."

"Your friends?"

"Well, they're sort of my friends. Em says I should stay away from them. That they could be dangerous. I don't think so, but—"

"If Em says they're dangerous, you should probably listen to her," I say.

"I know, I know," Luca says with faux exasperation. "But they started coming here just after I woke up. And they come when I call them. Like this." He slaps the water with a little more effort. "Just watch."

He slaps the water for another minute. I can see he's about to give up, but then something swirls just beneath the water, twenty feet out. I place a hand on Whipsnap.

"Luca," Adoni says, his tone serious and very adult sounding. He has one hand on his bolas and a knife already in the other.

"I know, I know," Luca says, waving away the man's concern.

I look to Krane. He's watching, too, but his arms are crossed and he looks only half-interested.

A puff of air brings my focus back to the swirling water. Something took a breath.

The swirling shape rises again, five feet closer. I can see a vague, large shape beneath the surface of the water. Had this been midday instead of sunset, I might have been able to see the true size of the creature, but the orange sun fails to pierce the water.

Again, five feet closer, the swirl emerges. As the creature surfaces, a cloud of expelled steam blocks its face for a moment. Then the air clears and a doglike face with big black eyes is revealed.

"Gloop!" I shout, charging into the water.

"Solomon?" Luca says, now sounding afraid.

"What's he doing?" I hear Adoni shout. I can hear his feet, too, running toward the beach.

I wrap my arms around the Weddell seal that has saved my life twice. The seal nuzzles against my side and then swims circles around me.

Adoni arrives, bolas spinning above his head.

"It's okay," I say, raising a hand up. "He's a friend."

"You're friends with this creature?" Adoni asks.

"Among others," I say.

He lowers the bolas. "Right. The dinosaurs."

"Grumpy is here, too?" I ask.

"Grumpy?"

"The male cresty."

Adoni starts to sound annoyed when he says, "Cresty?"

"The dinosaurs." I remember what Aimee called them. "The crylophosaurs."

"Ahh," Adoni says, finally understanding. "We have heard stories."

"Have you seen them?" I ask.

Adoni attaches the bolas to his belt with a shake of his head. "I've seen a lot of strange things, but you... I saw them just once. They left. With Xin."

Before I can ask for more details, a woman clears her throat behind Adoni. He falls silent and steps aside.

It's Kainda.

Gloop slides beneath the water and disappears.

"Go get something to eat," she says, then glances at Adoni and Krane. They nod and start away from the lake. "Take the kid, too."

Adoni takes Luca's hand and leads him away.

I take a step to follow them, but Kainda stops me with a stare and says, "You stay."

Luca glances back at me apologetically before fading into the jungle.

Standing in waist deep water, I'm not sure what to say to Kainda. Our interactions have been brief and intense. Em clearly trusts her, but last I knew, Kainda would have liked nothing better than to cave in my skull.

She glances over her shoulder, listening, and then turns back to me. As she walks toward the water's edge, her hand slides subtly down to the large stone hammer attached to her belt and unclips it.

Crap.

27

Not reaching for Whipsnap is a struggle. Kainda could crush my skull with a single hammer strike if I don't defend myself. But she helped Em and Luca escape from the Nephilim. And Em clearly trusts her. They've been fighting together, leading this ragtag group of hunters for months.

Xin's message repeats in my mind. Don't trust anyone.

But how can I do that? Even if it's a risk, I'm going to have to trust someone.

Em and Luca without a doubt.

But Kainda? Her ferocious reputation and past disdain for me make her the most likely candidate for betrayal. But it's *too* obvious. The moment she started acting funny, someone would notice. Especially me.

She grips the hammer and pulls it from her belt.

And this intimidation is exactly what I'd expect from Kainda. She's clearly made an effort to change, though. So I decide to risk trusting her. I hold my ground, but make no move to defend myself. *She won't hurt me,* I tell myself. *She's glad I'm alive, just like the rest of them.*

When she places the end of the hammer against my chest, I'm not so sure. Still, she has yet to bludgeon me. "You…" Her voice burns with contempt. "You changed everything." She shoves the hammer forward, knocking me back a little deeper in the water.

Kainda steps closer, moving out of the shade and into the orange glow of the setting sun. The light transforms her. Her skin looks soft. Her deep red hair tied back in a braid looks pretty. Her eyes, though they burn with intensity, make my insides twist. I'm no longer seeing a fellow hunter. I'm seeing a beautiful girl.

"Everything used to make sense to me," she says, nearly shouting. "The world made sense. Hunting. Killing. The Nephilim. *Everything.* Even hating you. You had everything I wanted, and then you took it all away. You destroyed it."

She shoves me again. It hurts, but it's bearable. And I'm still distracted by the new way I'm seeing her.

"You could have killed me," she says. "Could have let that cry-lophosaur kill me. That would have made sense. But now, I'm just confused. What felt right then, feels wrong now. I don't like it."

She's in my face now, like this is a WWF pre-match verbal smackdown. And she could probably intimidate any wrestler on TV. But I just stare into her eyes, listening, and trying to make sense of what I'm feeling. As much as she says I confused her world, she is doing the same to me now. Her strength, her passion and her beauty are making me forget that she is a killer and the daughter of Ninnis.

It's not her fault, I remind myself. She wasn't born hard. She was made that way, and she's proven her true strength by turning against it.

"Why?" she shouts. "Why didn't you kill me?"

When I don't answer, she takes a deep breath, lets out a sigh, and tilts her head to the water between us. When she does, I see a streak of silky jet-black hair in the center of her head. It's pulled back tight and mixed in with the braid, visible only from above.

Innocence reclaimed.

The sight of Kainda's black hair is the last straw. My intellect takes a back seat for a moment and my emotions guide my hand to Kainda's chin. I tilt her head up and two things surprise me. First, Kainda hasn't broken my hand. Second, I lean in quickly and plant my lips against hers. It's awkward at first. I've never done this before. In fact, I doubt Kainda has either. Hunters aren't interested in romance.

But then something changes. Our bodies relax. I wrap my arms around her, pulling her close. Her hammer drops from her hand with a plunk as it sinks beneath the water.

I'm not sure how long the kiss actually lasts. My mind normally keeps track of such minor details without any effort, but all sense of time is gone. When we finally do separate, she still has that dangerous edge about her—something I think I like—but all of her hostility toward me is gone.

Her shouted questions register, now that my intellect is free to think again. Why? Why didn't you kill me? "That's why," I say, realizing the truth for the first time. When I saved Kainda from the matriarch cresty named Alice, I was being driven by Ull, who, as it turns out, represents the majority of my emotional side. And Ull is now a part of me. Ull is me, and I him. No longer separate. Which means all of the feelings he had for Kainda, despite her aggression—or perhaps because of it—are my feelings now. I am undeniably attracted to her.

And apparently, the feeling is mutual.

A slight shift of brush by the shore sends both of us into action. We separate quickly. Whipsnap springs out as I pull the weapon from my belt. Kainda quickly recovers her hammer from beneath the water. We stand side by side and face...

Em. She's smiling and looks a little uncomfortable.

Busted.

"Umm," she says. "I just wanted to tell you. There's some food. If you want it."

Kainda and I just stand there. Looking at her. No one knows what to say. Hunters don't kiss. They don't have feelings for each other. But that's changing. Em loves me like a brother. Tobias loved her like a father. Those things aren't supposed to happen, either.

"I'll just..." Em takes a step back into the jungle. "We'll talk later."

Em disappears into the jungle and we're alone again. I slowly turn to Kainda. She's dripping wet from recovering her hammer, and she's standing there, ready for a fight that isn't going to come. She meets my gaze and I know I look equally silly because a glimmer of a smile creeps onto her face. That small smile is like a punch in the gut, but instead of wincing, I laugh.

Kainda's smile widens. It's not much, and it seems to confuse her, or at least the emotions accompanying it does, but it's something I never thought I'd see. I trudge back to shore and take a seat on a fallen tree. Kainda follows and I force my eyes to the ground so I don't get caught gawking. I have seen a number of hunters in my time underground and have never once noticed how little clothing we actually wear. And now I'm having trouble not noticing.

Being a teenager is so confusing.

Kainda takes a seat next to me. For several minutes, we watch the sun set. The light still stings my eyes some—midday is nearly unbearable without sunglasses—but the diffused light of the falling sun hits Kainda's high cheekbones in such a way that a little discomfort is worthwhile.

"So…" she eventually says, "you're friends with seals *and* dinosaurs?"

I'm about to ask how she knows about the cresties, when I remember she was there when the male cresty I named Grumpy allowed me to place my hand on his head. The small pack of predators later aided in her escape with Em.

"I don't understand it, either."

"What about the other things you can do?" she asks. "The wind. The storms."

"I can't do those things anymore," I say.

"I noticed," she says. "You wouldn't have had any trouble defeating the others."

That she excludes herself from those who would have been easy to defeat, by saying "the others," makes me smile. Her confidence, I'm realizing, is one of the things I like best about her.

I begin explaining about how my abilities faded when I entered Tartarus. This brings up all sorts of questions about that strange land, how I got out and how I managed to find the lake. From there, we work our way back. My birth. My life before. When Ninnis took me. How he broke me. And how my memory came back to me. We laugh a little when I recall the things I said to her as Ull, and she seems pleased that some of my insults were made by me pretending to be Ull.

Sometime during the conversation, our hands find each other. The contact is like a static spark. We both draw back quickly and share an awkward smile. Sure, we kissed, and holding hands is kind of a step backward, but the kiss was…passionate. Holding hands is somehow more intimate. Less guarded. It implies a stronger bond that cannot be forged so quickly, or so it would seem, through a kiss.

After an awkward moment of silence, I ask her about her life. The story is short and details scarce. But that's okay. I can fill in the blanks. She would have been broken at a young age. Molded really. She didn't need to forget her previous life. The underground realm was all she ever knew. Pain. Blood. Violence. She was steeped in it from birth. That she can sit here now, holding my hand, is nothing short of a miracle.

Her story shifts quickly to current events. The freed hunters, what they are calling the freemen, have been slowly organizing. Word is spreading, but recruitment is dangerous. If the invitee is not receptive, violence is guaranteed. They had been planning to reach out to the outside world, but every encounter with mankind has ended in violence, too. The men and women who have come to Antarktos, have come to fight.

"Not all of them," I say.

She looks at me, unbelieving. The sun is now down, but the light from the half moon and my now natural night vision make Kainda easy to see.

"I have friends," I say. "From my life before. They're here now. And I can't picture either of them wanting to hurt anyone."

"You saw them?" she asks.

"No." The answer discourages me. But I know they're here. I dig into my pack and pull out the bandanna. "This has Merrill's scent," I say.

Kainda takes the bandanna and smells it. Anyone from the outside world would think she was crazy, but it's normal behavior for a hunter. In the darkness of the underworld, many things are identified by scent long before sight.

I take out a single strand of blond hair. "This is Mira's."

Kainda takes the hair and sniffs it. "No scent." She looks it over. "It's the same color as your hair…but the texture is different. Rougher."

Kainda hands the hair and bandanna back to me. "This…Mira. She is the girl from the image you carried."

How does she know about that? She sees the question on my lips and answers. "My father spoke of it. Said she was your weakness. That you…loved her."

While things like love are foreign to hunters, jealously is not. And Kainda isn't very good at concealing it. But I'm no better at lying, so I tell the truth. "I did love her. I still do, I suppose. She means a lot to me. But twenty years have passed for her. She's a grown woman. Maybe with a husband. Children. Who knows? But I feel strongly about her father, Merrill, too. And Aimee, her mother."

"Aimee? Not the teacher?"

I'd left that detail out of my story, but if I'm trusting Kainda, I'm trusting Kainda. "Yes. She is Mira's mother. She helped deliver me when I was born."

"But...you took her. Gave her to the masters." Kainda looks confused, until she sees my downturned eyes. "She does not like me."

I recognize that Kainda is trying to lighten the mood, but she's not very good at it. She manages to change the subject.

"Mira. Did you ever..." Kainda places her fingers against my lips.

I smile. "No. Never. We bumped feet once."

Her forehead scrunches up. "You bumped *feet?*"

"Hey, it's kind of a big deal to a fourteen year old boy."

Kainda's jealously fades as she laughs at me. And I actually don't mind that she's laughing at me.

"They had a dog with them," I say. I hold up the bandanna. "That's the strong smell on this."

"What is a dog?"

Right. There are no dogs on Antarctica. "They're hairy. Four legs. A tail that wags when they're happy."

"Woof." Kainda does an impression of a dog barking. It's so spot-on that I know she's seen it. Seen them.

"That's it!" I say.

She points out at the water. "They crossed the lake toward

Olympus. Three days ago. The dog was with them. It made that noise when your—" She shakes her hand at the water, looking for the right word. "—other friends greeted them."

"The seals," I say. "Gloop."

"The seals. Yes."

I nearly ask if anyone spoke to them, but it's clear they didn't. "We have to find them."

"Because of her?" Kainda says.

"Because of all of them. Adoni thinks Aimee will be at Olympus, too. And they're our best chance at getting help."

She squeezes my hand. "We will find them together."

Knowing that Kainda, this infinitely dangerous woman who has somehow won my heart, will be by my side when I enter the Nephilim stronghold in search of Hades, and the Clark family, fills me with confidence.

A chill runs up my spine. At first, I think I'm cold, but the nighttime air is still a perfectly comfortable temperature. Then my mind catches up with my body. There's a scent in the air. It's subtle, but unmistakable.

Blood.

Nephilim blood.

28

A general rule of thumb for anyone trying to hide from Nephilim is: if you detect their presence, run away. Apparently, neither Kainda nor I, abide by this rule. Instead, we quickly determine the direction of the wind, and thus the direction from which the smell emanates, and run *toward* it. It's not because we have a death wish, it's because people we care about are nearby and in danger. At least, that's my motivation.

When Kainda says, "You should go back and warn the others," I know her motivation is the same.

It's the same reason why I won't abandon her now. Only one hunter has managed to kill a Nephilim before. Me. And that was with my abilities. If there is any hope of defeating whatever waits for us in the jungle, it is together. Kainda must realize the same thing, because she doesn't urge me to leave again.

We run, side by side, through the jungle. Fast and quiet. Concealed in the shadow of the canopy that, in the darkness of night, feels almost like the underground. As the scent of Nephilim blood grows stronger, we arm ourselves and slow our approach. Even hunters don't leap into battle without first knowing what they're facing.

A beam of moonlight streaks through a hole in the canopy, lighting a small clearing. At the center of the clearing is a shape I recognize. Krane. He's kneeling on the ground, head downturned like he's injured. Did Krane already face the Nephilim and lose? I step forward, intending to ask, but Kainda's firm grip on my shoulder stops me.

"Look at the ground," she whispers.

A ten foot circle of leaf litter has been cleared away to reveal smooth earth below. Strange symbols, like crop circles, have been etched into the soil around him.

"Is it a trap?" I ask.

"Worse," she says, tightening her grip on her hammer.

Krane begins to mumble, speaking Sumerian. I catch just a few words. "Fathers." "Hear me." "Come."

"What's he doing?" I ask.

Kainda looks about ready to explode. "Speaking to the Fathers."

"The Fathers?"

"The Nephilim Fathers."

My mind figures things out. Krane is speaking to demons!

"But why would—"

"I didn't think they were real," Kainda says, and I think she's talking to herself, but then she looks at me. "He is a shifter. A Nephilim who can look human."

The ramifications of this are vast. I've heard in the past that there are Nephilim living out in the world among the human race. I wondered how such a thing could be possible. Here is my answer. Krane the hunter, friend to Em and Kainda, is a Nephilim. I can't imagine what would have happened if he had been the one who held the knife when I placed it against my throat, instead of Tunis. But things could still get very bad. If he's trying to speak with the demon fathers, he is no doubt communicating my presence.

A purple glow radiates from the ground in front of Krane and I see a deep pool of purple blood.

"They're coming," Kainda says. "We must stop him. Now!"

Kainda charges from the jungle. I follow close behind. And despite our ferocious intent, we both remain silent. No battle cries. No hint of approach. Kainda raises her weapon, preparing to strike Krane's head. I shift the blade end of Whipsnap back, ready to strike with deadly force. If Krane is a Nephilim, there's no need for me to hold back.

Five feet from Krane, the wind shifts. He sucks in a surprised breath.

Kainda swings hard.

And misses.

Krane ducks beneath the blow and Kainda's momentum carries her beyond her target. Krane leaps up and spins around to face me, but he isn't prepared for where he finds me. I leapt from a rock and am now airborne. On a collision course. Krane jumps back, but Whipsnap's reach covers the distance. The bladed end arcs through the air, tracing a purple line down Krane's chest.

We both land and square off. The purple blood at the end of

Whipsnap's blade reveals the cut down Krane's torso to be an inch deep. Not a mortal wound for a Nephilim, but it's something. Kainda takes a fighting stance behind Krane. She catches my eye and somehow I understand what she's thinking. Our next attack will be as one. He cannot defend both sides.

We circle him slowly.

Tension builds as we prepare to attack.

Then I notice something strange. Krane's wound is not healing. Nephilim warriors heal from physical wounds very quickly. Shifters must be different. Which means that I don't need to hit this thing in the forehead to kill it. The wound catches my attention again. Not only is it not healing, it seems to be…growing.

"Something's not right," I say to Kainda.

"We're wasting time," she replies. Her voice is almost a growl.

I glance at the purple blood. The glow is fading. Whatever Krane was doing, we interrupted it. He needs to kill us to continue. So why isn't he attacking? Nephilim don't fear hunters. "He's tricking us," I say. "Wants us to get closer."

Krane laughs. His voice morphs from something human to something else. Something horrible. He slaps his hands against his chest, digs his fingers into the wound and takes hold of his flesh.

What the—

With a roar, Krane tears his chest open. Purple blood showers to the ground, forcing Kainda and I to leap back. The blood has healing properties, but in its pure form is so powerful, it can kill. Had we been closer, as I suspect he desired, we would have been coated in the stuff. I cringe, expecting to see an exposed ribcage and slippery organs, but what I see is far worse.

Krane's skin seems to explode away from him, falling like sheets of wet toilet paper. And his body...it grows. From within. His new skin is dark red and covered with scales. He grows taller. His already large muscles expand. It's as though a much larger creature had been compressed and was barely contained within a human shaped shell. He's now ten feet tall—just like the Nephilim skeleton Merrill uncovered by the wall. His face splits down the middle. The flesh slides away, teeth and all. An angular Nephilim face is revealed—yellow eyes, double rows of teeth and horn-like knobs on its forehead. In fact, he looks very devil-like.

"Lucifer?" I guess.

His eyes snap toward me. "Eshu," he says. "But you were close."

Eshu. I read about him once, which means I remember every one of the scant details provided about him. He's a trickster god—meaning he likes to fool people into harm's way, causing injury, personal loss, loss of faith and even wars. Eshu is the trickster god of the Yorùbá tribe in Nigeria. But he's not alone. There are many other trickster gods throughout history: Anansi, Lilith, Loki, Māui and like my initial guess, the most famous of them all, Lucifer. Satan. The Devil. While the warriors hold power among the Nephilim, it is the shifters who have had the most profound effect on the human race.

Eshu's next statement corrects that last assumption. He spits purple blood as he speaks. "Lucifer is my father."

My mind reels with this revelation. The demon, Lucifer, is not only real, but is this shifter's father. Granted, I knew the

Nephilim were the children of a coupling between human mothers and demon fathers, but I never put a name to the fathers, and for some reason, never *that* name.

While I try to make sense of this surreal revelation, my guard falls, and Eshu takes advantage. The big Nephilim is quick and agile. He leaps across the ground on all fours and tackles me around the waist before I can react. It's like getting struck by a charging polar bear. Stars dance in my vision when I strike the ground hard, but I still see Eshu's open maw as it approaches my neck. The double rows of sharp teeth will have no trouble tearing out my throat. I have just seconds to live.

Then I see Kainda, in the air above Eshu, hammer raised and ready to deliver a crushing blow.

But Eshu must have seen my eyes widen. He twists around with surprising speed and backhands Kainda in the side. Her body crashes into the jungle, stopping against the trunk of a tree.

"Kainda!" I shout.

My concern causes Eshu to laugh. "Hunters concerned for hunters. It's heart-warming. Really." He laughs again, turning his head to the sky with a howl that warriors use just before killing an enemy—me, in this case. Kainda won't recover in time to help me.

29

For all of Eshu's strength, speed and confidence, he has forgotten that the person he now faces is a hunter, trained by Ninnis and chosen of Nephil. I am not as weak as he seems to think. I put the time he spends mocking me to good use. Whipsnap never fell from my grasp. I slowly pull the weapon up. I turn the blade toward Eshu just as he throws himself down on top of me to finish the job. The blade pierces his chest, sinking ten inches deep.

For a moment, I think I've struck the killing blow. But he reels back and up onto his feet with a shout of pain. I cling to Whipsnap, and I'm pulled off the ground. I've impaled his breastplate and the blade can't slice through. Rather than give up my weapon, I hold on tight, dangling two feet off the ground.

But I don't want to be within Eshu's grasp when his senses return. I pull myself up, plant my feet against his waist, and use my leverage to bend the mace end of Whipsnap around. The spiked ball strikes Eshu in the face, crushing his red nose with a crunch.

Eshu flails back, but manages to take hold of my arm. His face is twisted with rage. I kick and pull, but I can't break free. I shove Whipsnap's blade in deeper, but the pain doesn't stop him. He opens his mouth, clearly intending to bite my arm off. The pressure on my wrist increases and I shout in pain. "Nephil was wrong, you are not strong at all."

At the moment, I agree with him. He's not even a full sized warrior, and though I've managed to injure him, I suspect the injuries will heal. The Krane skin he wore might not have, but I suspect that was intentional.

His breath tickles the skin of my arm. I close my eyes.

There's a sound like a whistle. Two whistles. And each is followed by a wet smack. My eyes snap open as Eshu roars in pain and drops me to the ground.

The shifter devil stumbles back. Two knives are buried in his eyes. The skill with which they were thrown identifies the attacker.

Em.

But she is not alone.

Bolas wrap around Eshu's feet, binding him in place. As he tears the knives out of his eyes, there's a battle cry that comes close to matching any Nephilim's. Kainda, now recovered, leaps at Eshu and brings her stone hammer down on his head with all of her strength. The crack of Eshu's skull breaking is loud. The monster falls to the ground, immobilized, but still alive. In fact, I can see the fresh wounds healing.

I stand above the fallen Nephilim and yank Whipsnap out of his chest. He coughs purple blood, smiles and looks at me through one of his now healed eyes. "You are nothing," he says.

"You," I say, interrupting the shifter. "Are about to die." I raise Whipsnap above my head. "You will cease to exist. So you see, Eshu, it is you, the Nephilim, who are nothing."

A look of fear stitches across his face a moment before I bring Whipsnap's razor sharp blade down, decapitating the monster.

I step away from the growing pool of purple blood, catching my breath. Kainda steps up next to me. "Now you've killed two of them."

"I had help," I admit.

"Yes," she says, looking at me with a look of satisfaction, "You did."

Em rushes up to us. Adoni inspects the scene.

"Are you all right?" Em asks.

Kainda huffs like it's a ridiculous question. I answer for both of us, "We're fine."

Adoni whispers something in another language, but I can tell by the sound that it's a curse. He's looking at half of Krane's shed face. His voice shakes with horror as he asks, "This was Krane?"

"A shifter," I say. "He was trying to speak to the fathers."

"A shifter?" Em says. "I didn't think—"

"Nor did I," Kainda says, her back to us as she stares into the jungle. "But they are real. And among us."

Trust no one. Xin's words now make sense. If a shifter can take human form, they can probably take *any* human form, even those of people I trust. But Kainda, Em and Adoni have proven themselves to me tonight through their actions.

"We need to leave," Adoni says. "If he made contact—"

"He didn't," Kainda says. "He had just begun the ritual."

Adoni stands, shaking his head. "It doesn't matter. The Fathers will know he tried to initiate contact. They will know that his ritual was interrupted. And they will know the mission with which he was tasked. They will come for him. His blood will be easy to track."

"We'll head underground," Em says. "We've planned for this."

Em is right. The hunters need to flee. It is not yet time to strike. Our numbers are too few, and we need help from the outside world. But I cannot join them. Not while the Clarks are here, and in danger. And not until I find Hades and the Jericho Shofar.

"Go," I say. "But I cannot go with you."

"What? Why not?" Em says quickly, a hint of anger rising in her voice.

"I need to go to Olympus."

"His friend is there," Adoni says, but he's not defending me. "The teacher."

"Aimee?" Em says. She met Aimee once, in the Norse library. She knows how much Aimee means to me.

"Solomon, you can't—"

"Mira is here, too. And Merrill."

Like with Aimee, Em knows all about Mira and Merrill. She knows about the photograph. About the note that Mira left behind for me. She knows.

"Sol…"

"I also need to find Hades," I say.

Adoni staggers back, eyes wide with fear. "Hades! *Why?*"

"He is not like the others," I say.

"No," Adoni says. "He is *far* worse."

His fear begins to infect me. I can't let it. "It doesn't matter. Cronus said he would help us."

Adoni is confused. "Cronus?"

"The Titan," I say.

"You met...a Titan?"

"In Tartarus." My patience wears thin. "It's a long story and we don't have the time. But I need to find Hades." I look at Em. "And I need to save my friends. Both are at Olympus."

"I'm going with him," Kainda says, attaching her hammer to her belt and crouching by the purple pool of blood. She takes a leather wineskin and carefully scoops up some of the blood.

Collecting Nephilim blood strikes me as revolting. My nose crinkles in disgust and I ask, "What are you doing?"

Kainda caps the skin and wipes away the blood on the outside with a leaf. "It saves lives," Kainda says. "It could save yours."

I can tell she finds it as revolting as me by the way she pinches the skin between two fingers and quickly ties it to her belt. She'd rather not be taking it, but she's right. The blood could save a life. At least the Nephilim are good for something.

"Then I'm coming, too," Em says.

"Em," I say, shaking my head.

"You can't," says Adoni.

"What about Luca?" I ask.

She turns to Adoni. "Take Luca and the others underground. Six groups. Six different paths. When you reach the gathering place, wait for us."

I raise my voice. "No, Em, you need to stay—"

"She needs to come," Kainda says. She bends down to Eshu's severed head and yanks out the knife still buried in his eye. "We need her help."

I know how impossibly hard that admission is for Kainda to make. So hard, in fact, that it quickly convinces me she's right. I sigh. "Adoni, do as she says. We will find you."

Adoni looks like he might argue, but he's outnumbered three to one. And, I suspect, he's outranked by Em, Kainda and now by me. He bows in defeat and backs toward the jungle.

"Adoni wait," I say. "When we meet you next, do not trust us until…" Until what? I know what I want to say. We need some kind of password system that only the four of us know, just in case one of us is replaced by a shifter. My solution is ridiculous, but without context, they'll never know. I raise my hand and do my best Vulcan greeting, opening my fingers, two to each side, and say, "Live long and prosper."

He looks at me like I've gone crazy. Maybe he has seen Star Trek? "It's what I'll say the next time we meet. So you'll know I'm not—" I nod to Eshu's dead body. "—one of them."

He nods his head in understanding. "Ahh."

"And you," I say. "Will do this." I reverse my two center fingers so that they come together, leaving just the index and pinky fingers extended. "Nanu nanu."

Adoni raises his hand, performs the gesture perfectly and says, "Nanu nanu."

I nearly laugh, hearing someone here say Robin Williams's greeting from Mork & Mindy, but I contain my humor. "Perfect,"

I say. "Now go."

As Adoni leaves, Em calls after him, "Tell Luca I love him."

Adoni waves in response, then fades into the dark jungle.

I turn to Kainda and Em. "Thank you. For coming."

Kainda rolls her eyes and stomps off in the direction of Olympus. "I hope you're not going to talk the whole way there."

Em smiles at me and pats my shoulder. "You have strange taste, brother." Then she follows after Kainda.

I take one last look at Eshu's body. It took four hunters to kill the ten foot tall Nephilim. And now the three of us are heading into the core of the Nephilim world, where thirty foot giants reside. But my friends are there, too, and they have no idea what waits for them.

I'm coming, Mira, I think. I know there can never be anything between us, but she stole a part of my heart a long time ago, and never gave it back. She will always be important to me. If she and Merrill are here to find Aimee, they're here because of me. If something happens to any of them… I'm pretty sure I would drown under the weight of that burden.

With renewed urgency, I run into the jungle. As I pass Em and Kainda, they give chase. The Clarks have a three-day head start, but I doubt they can travel as quickly as three conditioned hunters. We'll gain ground quickly. And if we can catch them before they reach Olympus, we might be able to save them. If not…

I'm coming.

30

We run for the rest of that night and half of the following day. We hear occasional bouts of distant gunfire. Twice, we cross strong cresty scent trails and steer clear. We don't fear the dinosaurs, but they could delay us. That said, while we might be hunters and conditioned for long distance runs, we can't run forever.

I slow my pace when I see a group of boulders that will conceal us as we rest. I test the area with my nose. There are a thousand subtle smells, including blood, smoke, fresh-cut wood and gunpowder, but most of them are carried by the wind. We have been moving steadily upward for several hours now and the wind rolls down-slope, carrying the scents of Olympus with it.

Satisfied that there's no danger lurking nearby, I settle down next to a rock and lean my head back. Em slides over the rock and sits next to me. She's out of breath, like me, but she's also covered in sweat.

She looks at me and frowns. "You're not even sweating."

I look down at myself. She's right. I'm definitely feeling the effects of running so far, though. I'm exhausted. And hungry. My lack of perspiration can wait. Em seems to be thinking the same thing. She takes out a wrapped cloth, opens it and hands me a stick of dried meat. I don't even ask what it is. I just eat it, chase it down with a drink from my water skin and rest my head.

Then I open my eyes. "Where's Kainda?"

Kainda replies from above. "Up here."

I turn my eyes up and see Kainda further up the incline.

"You two rest. I'm going to scout ahead." She doesn't wait for an acknowledgement or for approval. She just turns and goes.

"She's a machine," I say.

"What's a machine?" Em asks.

"Something man-made. Out of metal usually. They can move for a long time, and are stronger than men."

"Then yes, she *is* a machine."

We share a smile and Em gets serious. "Why her?"

I know she's talking about Kainda. She saw us kiss. For a moment, I'm terrified that I've read our relationship all wrong, that Em sees me as something different than a brother. She did pretend to be my wife, after all. "What do you mean?" I ask, suddenly nervous. "You don't—you aren't...interested in—"

"Oh! No!" She looks like she's just tasted something foul or licked a frog. "Ugh. Gross."

"Okay! Okay!" I say, laughing.

She shakes her head at me and takes a bite of dried meat. "Gross."

I lean my head back on the stone, returning my thoughts to

her question. "I don't know," I admit.

"Aside from the obvious," Em says, then makes an hourglass motion with her hands.

I laugh again. It's nice to have an open conversation. I can speak more freely with Em than I have with anyone in the past. "When I...you know..."

Em places her fingers against her lips.

"Right," I say. "It was instinct. It felt right."

Em nods. If there is anything a hunter understands, it's instinct.

"I just saw her hair, and—" That was it. Kainda is beautiful, and has other qualities that attract me to her—confidence and strength, but what makes her irresistible is that black streak in her hair. While there are many other hunters who have shrugged off the Nephilim, Kainda's bonds were tighter than most. "I had Aimee," I say. "You had Tobias. And he had Luca. Our connections helped us escape. We didn't have to do it alone. Kainda was born here. She was raised by Ninnis. Can you imagine?"

I can see by the look in Em's eyes that she can't.

"She not only defied her master, Thor, one of the most powerful Nephilim warriors, but she also defied Ninnis, the most skilled hunter in the underworld. She knew nothing but the life of a hunter, and never once experienced what it meant to be loved. And yet, here she is, freed from captivity because of her own courage."

I look at Em. She nods.

"She deserves love."

"You're right," Em says. "Just try not to make her upset."

I'm about to offer some kind of witty reply, but instead say, "What I can't figure out is, why me? I mean, aside from the obvious." I give my muscles a flex and raise my eyebrows a few times.

Em sticks out her tongue like she's throwing up and we share a laugh. Then she gets serious. "I think her reasons are probably similar to yours." She leans forward, takes my hair and pulls it around to where I can see it. "You're free. Totally free. No hunter has ever done that before. I don't think anyone has even considered the possibility. I know I hadn't."

"The burden was lifted in Tartarus," I say. "I didn't do it by myself."

"Doesn't really matter how it happened," she says. "Only that it did."

I look at the ground, wondering if that's all there is to it. Is Kainda attracted to my freedom or to me?

Em seems to sense my thoughts and adds, "Plus she probably likes your, you know—" She flexes, and her muscles, while a little smaller than mine, are quite impressive. She laughs, but then grows serious. "Also, she was…offered to you. As a wife. By her father. Hunters take that seriously. It's kind of an unsaid thing, but marriage is the only real relationship hunters are allowed. The coupling is supposed to be about producing stronger children."

"Selective breeding," I say. When she looks at me oddly, I know she doesn't understand. "It's what the outside world calls it. They do it with livestock. To create stronger animals."

"Exactly. They want stronger hunters. But some pairs bond—" she pauses, searching for the word. "Emotionally. Though it is hidden, and no one would ever admit it. But it's there. Kainda was offered to you by her father. You have been bonded."

The idea that I'm part of some ancient hunter arranged-marriage situation makes me a little sick to my stomach. But it still doesn't make sense. "Kainda doesn't seem like the kind of person to let customs dictate what she does."

"She is a hunter in every way, Sol. She would take the arrangement seriously."

I frown, a little disappointed by the idea that Kainda's interest is merely the product of custom.

Em lets out a gentle laugh. "But that doesn't explain her affection. It is most certainly not part of the arrangement."

I'm about to ask more when Kainda skids to a stop above us. My face flushes as I think we've been caught talking about her, but Kainda quickly says, "I found something. I think we're close."

She heads off, back up the rise. We chase after and don't stop until we near the crest of the hill. The smells hit me first. Blood—human and Nephilim. Modern weapons. Old Spice.

"They were here," I say.

"Not long ago," Kainda says. "The body is not yet rotting."

Body!?

I rush to Kainda as she squats next to a body. The man's limbs are mangled and it looks like he might have been folded at the waist—in the wrong direction. He's got a shaved head and wears military fatigues. The patch on his arm identifies him as a British soldier. His weapon, a modern looking rifle, lies a few feet away, bent and broken. A large knife is sheathed on his belt.

"Do you know him?" Kainda asks.

"No," I say. "But he must have been with them."

Em surprises me by taking the man's knife. She sees my confused look and says, "I'll avenge him with it." She attaches the knife to her belt, adding it to her collection. She keeps the knives around her waist and attached to two crisscrossing bands that form an X over her chest. The man's knife is larger than all the rest, but it fits her ensemble nicely.

"There are tracks," Kainda says.

We quickly split up, following the group of tracks as they lead down the other side of the hill. Bullet casings litter the area. More dried Nephilim blood. They were putting up a good fight by the looks of it. Some of the paths lead further downhill, but two of them end. Three if you count the Nephilim that attacked them.

Em and Kainda join me at the scene. There is dry human blood on a stone. Not much of it, which is good. There's a lot more dried Nephilim blood. And something else, so subtle I nearly miss it. It looks like purple dust. I reach a hand out.

"Don't touch that," Kainda warns.

"Why? What is it?"

"The powder will knock you unconscious if you inhale it," Em says. "On your skin, it will sap your strength."

"They were taken," Kainda says. "Alive."

I look at the evidence. The scuff marks. The positioning of human and Nephilim footprints. The boot sizes. The blood. Merrill's scent still lingers. He was one of the two, which leaves no doubt in my mind that Mira left the smaller boot prints. I recreate the scene. Mira fell and hit her head. She was confronted by a Nephilim. Merrill came to her aid. And if Em is right, they were both knocked unconscious and taken. "But…"

Em and Kainda look at me. "If they were taken, where are the tracks?"

The three of us scour the area. The big Nephilim's footprints are easy to spot, and where he came from is clear. But how he left…

"It's like he flew away," Em says.

Kainda scoffs. "The masters *cannot* fly."

No one argues, though I'm no so sure. The Gigantes in Tartarus had no trouble flying. And the scorpion-like tail in the thinker lab hinted that experiments had been done using attributes of the old Nephilim.

Before I have time to consider the possibilities, gunshots echo in the distance. The staccato picks up and I can hear Nephilim shouting war cries. A battle is being fought nearby. I intend to join it.

I break into a sprint, heading downhill toward the sound of a river. The trees thin and I catch a glimpse of a tall mountain just a few miles away. But it's more than a mountain. It's a city, built right into the stone, or carved out of it. I slow, looking at the amazing structure. It's stunning and horrifying.

"Olympus," I say.

Kainda and Em slow and look. "I've never seen it like this," Kainda says, her voice sharing a little bit of the awe I feel.

Em brings us back to reality, saying, "It's a horrible place."

With that, I turn my head downward and start to run. The sound of the river is louder and I can smell the moisture in the air. Once we reach the river, we can—

The ground shakes. A boom louder than anything I've ever heard rolls past. We stumble, fall and slide to a stop just as the shaking fades. The river is just twenty feet bellow.

"What was that!?" Em shouts.

Kainda is quick to her feet, hand on hammer, looking for danger.

I, on the other hand, sit still and listen. That was an explosion. A very large one. And explosions that big can have aftereffects. A distant roar confirms my fear. As it grows louder, I stand and motion for Kainda and Em to run away. "Run! Get higher!"

"*What?*" Kainda is offended that I would retreat. "Why?"

"The river!" I shout. The roar nearly drowns out my voice. "It's flooding! Run!"

As I run, I look to the side and see a wall of water tearing through the jungle, heading straight for us.

31

There's no time to run up the hillside, so we take to the trees instead, climbing the tall trunks like chimps. We reach the canopy just before the water hits. The roar beneath us sounds like Behemoth—powerful and hungry. I move across the canopy, trying to reach the river's edge and maybe get a glimpse of what's happening.

The trees shake when the water strikes. I lose my grip and fall a few feet, but catch myself. The fall didn't feel dangerous, but when I look down, I realize I nearly lost my life. I'm dangling over the river with no other branches beneath me. It's a fifty-foot fall into a raging torrent. The river has grown and expanded into the jungle on either side, and if I fell, it's possible that I'd be swept into a tree and knocked unconscious—if not snapped in half. Either way, I'd likely drown. I pull myself back up as the water deepens and speeds up.

Looking upriver, I see a frothing crest of water perhaps twenty feet tall, rushing through the trees. This is going to get worse before it gets better. "Hold on!" I shout, but I don't think anyone can hear me above the water's roar.

I swing myself up onto a branch and wrap my arms and legs around it like I'm a sloth. The water approaches as though in slow motion. I can't take my eyes off it. It's a force of nature. Seeing the water reminds me of the flooded underworld. Had the rushing waters looked like this? I decide against it. With so many underworld species now flourishing on the surface, they had time to get out. But Behemoth, trapped underground, found its chamber slowly flooded and eventually drowned.

A speck on the crest of the approaching wave catches my attention. There are trees and other debris pushed by the raging waters, but this object has the distinctive shape of a boat. A wooden boat. And it rides the wave like a surfer. *How is it not being smashed into the jungle*, I wonder, and then I see a man—a human—at the back, guiding the thing with a large rudder. The craft looks like an unfinished yacht without a mast. It stretches at least twenty-five feet. But it's also clearly not designed for people. Instead, I suspect it's something closer to a Nephilim rowboat, designed to carry just two of the giants. But to what?

My question fades as I look at the other passengers. There is a thin man with tan skin whose uniform I recognize as Chinese. A survivor of the Nephilim attack? Another looks to be Arab, but I'm not sure and then there is a black woman. But she's not dressed in military clothing like the rest, she's—Aimee!

The boat is swept beneath me and I see her face. And next to her—Merrill! A blond mop of hair whips my head toward the center of the boat so fast that I nearly fall out of the tree.

Mira.

Seeing her face brings tears to my eyes. *My old friend...* I thought I'd never see her again. Or Merrill. And yet, they're all here and reunited. How they managed to find each other and escape Olympus is beyond me. But they did it.

I hear voices rise up from below.

"Whitney!" It's the man at the rudder. His face looks Hispanic. His clothing is black. Military. U.S. I'd guess. "How are we doing, chica?"

I'm surprised when it's Mira who replies. "Keep to the left, Cruz."

Their voices fade as the craft moves past.

I shout to them, desperate. "Mira! Merrill! Aimee! Up here!"

My voice is lost in the roar of the river.

For a moment, I think they're looking at me, but they're not. They're looking beyond me. At the sky.

What are they watching for?

The boat is carried quickly away, and if the man, Cruz, can keep them in the middle of the river, they won't slow until reaching the lake.

With my friends out of reach, my thoughts return to the question of why Mira responded to the name, Whitney. Did she change her name? Was it some kind of military code name? Her middle name? None of these possibilities rings true. Then what?

She called the man Cruz, which is a common Hispanic last name. So he was probably using her last name, too. *Whitney.* Mirabelle Whitney, not Mirabelle Clark. *She's married.* The answer fills me with jealously and anger.

Granted, I knew she would be older than me, and that there was a possibility of her being married, or even being a mother. But the reality of it hurts. It's not like she was ever my girlfriend. I didn't even know her that long. But her photo carried me for so long that I guess I became attached. And her being married, for some strange psychological reason, feels like a betrayal. She lived her life without me.

And that means everyone else did, too.

Merrill.

Justin.

My parents.

They all lived on without me. They all went to parties. Saw movies. Vacationed. Laughed. Loved.

Without me.

The realization stings.

I know it's selfish, but I can't stop it.

I can't, but something else can. A shadow. It moves across the river so quickly that I'm not sure I actually saw something. How could a shadow fall on the river, anyway?

If it were flying, I realize, turning my head up.

It's just a speck when I see it, circling like some kind of predatory bird. But it looks far too high, which means it's also quite large. Hanging onto my perch with one hand, I take out my telescope and extend it using my teeth. With the spectacle to my eye, I try to find the airborne figure. It takes some time to zero in on the moving target, but when I do, I gasp.

Enki.

With the wings of a Gigantes.

And the tail of Cronus the Titan.

The thinkers somehow managed to imbue the Nephilim warriors with attributes previously held only by the eldest of their kind. *That's how they're going to reach the world*, I realize. Antarctica might now reside at the equator, but an ocean still separates the continent from the rest of the world.

They're going to fly to the mainland. I remember the small boat. The river is now deep enough to carry much larger vessels. *Maybe they'll even sail to the mainland?*

Enki is brother to Enlil. Together, they are the sons of Nephil and kings of the Sumerian Nephilim, the most ancient and powerful warrior clan. Next to Nephil, who now resides in Ninnis's body, they are the rulers of the underworld, commanders of a supernatural force beyond the comprehension of mankind.

So the question is, why is Enki here?

As he swoops downriver, the answer is clear. He's after the Clarks. Why he's after them is beyond me, and frankly, unimportant. What is important is that the Clarks escape. That doesn't seem likely if Enki is tracking them though.

I glance to the right, looking up river. Olympus rises high into the sky. Hades is there and the secret resting place of the Jericho Shofar with him. My answers and perhaps the only hope of defeating the Nephilim wait to the right.

To left are the Clarks. My friends. And they're about to face Enki on their own.

The decision is easy.

I'm nothing if not loyal.

I slide to the side of the branch, hanging by one arm. If I can keep myself afloat in the middle of the raging river, I should arrive at the lake just minutes after the Clarks. I might not be able to reach them in the water, but if Enki sees me, I have no doubt he'll forget all about the Clarks.

I let go.

My fall snaps to a stop after just a few inches. A vice grip of pressure sends a wave of pain down my arm. I'm pulled up until I come face to face with a very angry hunter.

"What are you doing?" Kainda says. She's standing on the branch and holding onto one above her with her free hand. That she's strong enough to lift me up with one arm is impressive. Unlike Em, Kainda has muscles that match mine.

Em slides through the canopy and joins us. The look of concern means she didn't see Kainda catch me. She only knows that Kainda is holding me out over the river. But her trust in Kainda is evident. She doesn't draw a knife. She simply says, "What happened?"

Kainda either doesn't hear the question or ignores it. She has some of her own. "Why were you leaving?"

Before I can think of a good reply, she comes up with an answer herself. "Just one look at her and you were going to leave! I—we mean so little to you?"

Em inches closer. "What are you talking about?"

"Mira." Kainda says the name with disdain. "And the teacher, Aimee. They just passed in a ship."

Em's eyes widen. "Is this true?"

"Yes," I say, and try to explain, but Em interrupts.

"And you were leaving?" I can hear the sting of betrayal in her voice too.

I sense that Kainda is about to speak again so I shout, "Shut up! Both of you!"

Kainda allows me to stand on the branch. My wrist is sore from where she gripped it, but I can't rub it with my other hand without falling from the branch. So I ignore the pain and say, "Yes, the Clarks just went by in a boat. Merrill was with them. And three other men. Soldiers, I think."

Em interrupts with, "But why—"

"Enki!" I shout, freezing both of them in place. "Enki was following them! And they don't stand a chance unless I go help! I know Hades is near, but they are my friends and I never—" I look into Kainda's eyes, "—*never* abandon my friends."

I look to Em. She nods, understanding.

I don't wait for Kainda to say whether she understands. We can work it out later. Right now, the Clarks need my help. I swing down on the branch, take a look at the river below, and let go. The cold water envelops me and yanks me forward. As I surface, I hear two splashes behind me. I spin and find Kainda and Em swimming toward me, closing the distance. I catch Kainda's eyes and mouth, "Thank you."

In response Kainda swims past me and says, "She better be worth it."

32

The river is a battle. We're making ground fast. Probably too fast. Every tree and boulder carries a potential death sentence. The key is to stay in the middle, where the water was already deepest, but even here there are dangers, exhaustion being the first. Swimming in placid water can be tiring, even just treading water. I went to a summer camp once. They had a pool with a deep end. To swim in the deep end you had to pass a test—tread water with just your feet for one minute, while holding a brick.

I tried three times. I never passed.

This…is harder.

The brick has been replaced by the weight of Whipsnap around my waist. Kainda carries the weight of her stone hammer. And Em, who is the smallest of us, carries countless knives around her waist and across her chest. I'm not sure how long we've been swimming. It's hard to keep track of time while trying not to be impaled, bludgeoned or drowned. But my arms are burning from the effort and I'm pretty sure my legs will turn to jelly if I try to walk. If we manage to catch up to the Clark family, I'm not sure how much use any of us are going to be.

I look at Kainda. Her brow is furrowed with determination, but her lips are shivering.

I'm about ten feet ahead of her, so when I ask, "Are you okay?" I have to shout.

She just glares back at me, not because she's angry about what we're doing, but because I asked the question. I'm no mind reader, but Kainda is easy to understand.

Behind Kainda, Em has the same look on her face. The look of a hunter. These two women are dangerous. If only my parents could see me now, floating down a raging river with two of the most dangerous women on Antarctica, if not the planet, racing toward an encounter with a half-human, half-demon worshiped as a god in the ancient world. I'm not sure they would call me 'Schwartz' anymore. Doesn't quite fit like it used to.

A spear of brown moving behind Em catches my attention. It's a large tree trunk and it actually looks like it was logged—no roots, no branches—rather than pulled over by the flooded river. Why the Nephilim would be cutting down trees, I have no idea. Nor do I care. I'm more focused on the respite the twenty-foot hunk of wood promises.

I point toward the approaching tree trunk. "Grab hold of it!"

Both women look at me like I better not be thinking they need a rest, which I'm sure they do, so I come up with another reason. "It's streamlined. Moving faster than us. We'll make better time."

This seems to make sense to Kainda and Em, or at least provides an acceptable excuse, and when the log catches up, they

230 THE LAST HUNTER - ASCENT

both grab hold. The log pulls them closer to me and I grab hold too, careful not to pull too hard and roll it. Kainda is on the other side of the log. Em is to my right. No one says a word. Hunters or not, they're exhausted. We hold on and let the river take us.

But it's not long before the river slows and widens. "We're nearing the lake," I say.

"Do you see them?" Em asks.

I can't see anything with my head just above water. "We need to get to shore." I push off the log and my body groans as I begin to swim. Em and Kainda follow without complaint, but none of us are moving too quickly. The river merges with the jungle. Where once there was a shoreline, there is now an endless pool of foot-deep water.

Reaching the shallows of the jungle, I get my feet beneath me and stand.

And then fall.

My legs are all but useless.

Thinking of Mira, I pull myself up again, using a tree for support.

"I don't think we're far from the lake," Em says. She's leaning against a tree, too. "I recognize the trees here."

Kainda stands behind her, relying on just her legs to hold her up. I suspect the strength that holds her up has more to do with internal fortitude than the power of her muscles. "It's not far," she confirms, pointing down river. The canopy stretches for perhaps two hundred feet, casting the flooded jungle in shade. Beyond that, I see slivers of blue light where the tree line ends and the lake begins.

I take a furtive step and my leg wobbles. But I stay up. I yank Whipsnap from my belt and place the heavy mace end in the water, using it to support my weight as I've done before.

"Lead the way, old man," Kainda says.

I'm too tired and focused on the Clarks to offer some kind of retort, so I just set out for the lake, moving as quickly as I can without collapsing. Our approach is clumsy and loud as we splash through the floodwaters. But I suspect time is short. Fifty feet from the lake's edge, I'm moving at a fast hobble. I hear voices in the distance. Shouts.

A shadow flickers over the canopy. No! I'm too late!

I try to run, but fall, landing in the shallow water.

Kainda grabs my arm and yanks me up. We keep moving.

There's an explosion, muffled by water. I move faster. The blinding shimmer of sunlight on water is just ahead.

In the distance, Enki's deep voice is speaking.

I slash at some branches blocking our path and then lunge through, reaching the lake's edge. I see the boat, far out in the lake, but no movement on board. But the boat holds my attention for just a moment. Between the shore and the boat, fifty feet above the water, is Enki. His bat-like wings beat at the air, keeping him aloft. And his long, scorpion tail twitches back and forth like an angry cat's. His head hair, which isn't covered by any kind of helmet, billows in the wind. He looks huge, and frightening, and he's dressed for war in ornate metal armor. What human military force could face down a monster like Enki, let alone army of them, and not simply run in fear?

An army of hunters, I think. But then I see Mira, clutched in his hands. She's speaking to him. Her words are lost over the distance, but the tone is angry and defiant. She has grown into a strong woman. Like Em. Like Kainda. But in the hands of a Nephilim like Enki, her defiance will soon be crushed out of her.

I fill my lungs to scream, hoping to pull Enki's attention away from Mira.

But then the giant flinches.

Mira falls from Enki's grasp as he paws at his breastplate.

What's happening?

"Mira!" I shout, but my voice is drowned out by a thunderous explosion.

Enki's body bursts from the inside out. Purple blood and guts shoot out of his exposed back. One of his wings tears free and the other dangles from the one remaining shoulder. His torso bursts and his head sails away in chunks. The breastplate that had been covering his chest shoots away so fast that I think I understand what happened. While Enki held her, she must have placed an explosive between his chest and breastplate. The force of the explosion, confined between the hard metal and his softer body, took the path of least resistance and tore him to pieces.

Mira killed Enki!

My surprise and pride are short-lived because it seems she also killed herself. The fifty-foot drop alone would hurt, but the force of the explosion adds some kick to her fall and she's propelled into the water. The remains of Enki's massive body crashes into the lake beside her with an explosion of white foam that hides Mira's landing site.

I yell her name again and wade deeper into the lake.

A tight grip on my arm stops me. It's Kainda. "Let me go!" I shout.

"You can't make it," Em says, backing up Kainda's silent, but forceful protest. "You're too weak and she's too far."

"She was…admirable," Kainda says. "But her fate is sealed."

"No!" I shout, yanking away. I push deeper into the water, but my legs falter and I fall to my knees. They're right. I can't save her. After all this time, Mira returned to Antarktos, and I couldn't get to her in time. I couldn't save her. "NO!"

I pound my fists on the water, taking my anger out. As I bring my fists up again, a ripple in the lake catches my attention. A gray dog-like face surfaces. Gloop! I slide in deeper and the seal swims up to me. I look into his big black eyes. "Go get her. Do you understand? Go! Save her!" I motion my hands to where Mira fell. "Go!"

And he does. The seal spins around, moving through the water like a missile. He cruises out into the deep water, leaping occasionally, and then he disappears beneath the surface. I stand waist deep in the water, dripping wet, breathing hard, waiting and watching.

"Solomon," Em says, sounding defeated.

"He can do it," I say, clinging to hope.

Nearly a minute passes.

Kainda places a hand on my arm, gently this time.

"He knows what he's doing," I say. "He saved me. He—"

The water far out on the lake, where Mira fell, ripples. A body rises, identifiable by the dark skin and hair as blond as mine. Mira. Gloop's body rises beneath hers like a living floatation device. The pod of seals rises with him, like escorts.

"They did it," Kainda whispers.

I look at her and say, "Never give up hope."

In response, she takes my hand, lacing our fingers together, and squeezes.

"Where are they taking her?" Em asks as the seals head further into the lake.

At first, I'm confused. I had assumed Gloop would bring her to me. But they're definitely heading away. Then I see the boat far in the distance. The seals are following the boat. "They're taking her home," I say. "To her family."

As I watch Mira fade into the distance with the seals, Kainda says, "Do you want to go with them? To your home? Your family?"

She's right, I know. If I caught up with the boat, I could be reunited with the Clarks. And they could probably get me back to the United States. But my home in Maine is now the North Pole and it's likely frozen over. And my parents could be dead. But even if none of that were true, my answer would remain the same.

"No," I say, looking at Kainda. "I *am* home." I look at Em. "I *am* with family."

I see flashes of uncommon emotion on both hunters' faces, but the expressions are erased by the sound of running feet splashing through water. We turn to face the threat. The hunter known as Tunis, who first put his trust in me, who Em claimed was one of their best, emerges from the jungle. He is weaponless and covered with long, bleeding slices—the kind made by a sword. Kainda catches the man by his shoulders.

"Tunis!"

He shouts in surprise, but then sees the three of us and looks relieved.

"Tunis," Em says. "What happened? Where is Luca?"

"Luca is safe. Underground with Adoni. And the others," Tunis says, his voice shaking. "I stayed behind with Marko, Selize and Annon to make sure they weren't followed."

"Where are the others?" Kainda asked.

"He found us," Tunis said.

"Who found you?" I ask, fearing the answer.

Tunis turns his nose to the air and sniffs. "He's here. He's here now!"

Tightening my grip on Whipsnap, I say, "*Who* is here?"

His eyes are wide. His arms shake. "Ninnis," he says. "Ninnis is here!"

33

A flock of birds shoots from the trees behind us, rising into the sky like a fast moving cloud. Pain grips my eyes as I look up into the bright blue sky. I squint as something moves across the sun. A splash spins me around toward the lake. I see nothing but a few ripples of water. Did he throw something? Is he trying to distract us?

The four of us stand back to back. I quickly hand Tunis the knife he'd previously held to my throat. It isn't much, but it's something. Em hands him a second, the big knife she took from the dead British soldier's body.

"The others that stayed behind with me are dead," Tunis says quickly. "He killed them all. In seconds."

Ninnis is a skilled hunter, perhaps the most skilled hunter. But killing three hunters in just a few seconds doesn't seem possible, even for him. At least, I hope it's not.

Em, Kainda and I stay quiet, weapons ready. This would be a difficult fight on our best day, but right now, we're exhausted and in no shape to do battle. But we do our best to look strong and not appear weak.

"He's not human," Tunis says. "He's—"

"Quiet," Kainda hisses.

Tunis falls silent, but I can still hear his shaky breathing, and I'd almost prefer he kept talking. It takes a lot to rattle a hunter like Tunis, and he seems petrified.

The seconds wear on.

I jump back as something rises from the water. It's the shape of a man. Scraggly deep red hair. The thin, sinewy body of a strong old man. He shakes his head like a dog, clearing the water from his face.

Then he stops with a quick intake of air. His eyes locked on me.

Ninnis.

His eyes widen for just a moment, but I can see that he had no idea I was here.

"Ull," he says, his voice lacking the menace I expected. "You... How?"

"You know how, Nephil," I say, addressing the spirit I believe is controlling him.

Ninnis grins his nearly toothless grin. "As with you, Solomon, our Lord Nephil, found my will too strong to control. It is *I* who controls him."

The idea is so ridiculous that I can't imagine any reason why Nephil would make such a claim. "Then set him free," I say. "You can end all of this. Right now."

"I might not give Nephil my body, but I still serve the will of the Nephilim," he says. His body shakes for a moment, like there is something inside, trying to escape, but he grits his teeth and contains it. "Lord Nephil wants you back. But that is no longer possible. It is *I* who now leads the Nephilim out into the world. And it is I who will be remembered for ending the days of men. But you will be a distraction for Nephil. I will, of course, have to kill you, as I should have before you... How *did* you escape Tartarus?" His eyes drift to my hair. I think he's just now noticed it. For a moment he seems stunned, which is understandable. To a hunter, my purified hair is an impossibility. "How did you...?"

"My burden was lifted," I say. "Cronus showed me how."

Mentioning Cronus's name brings a physical reaction to Ninnis's face. He shouts in pain and something writhes beneath his skin. He shouts angrily and regains control.

Kainda nearly moves in to strike, but Em stops her.

Ninnis sneers at Kainda. "Come, traitorous daughter! I will gladly strike you down first!" But he doesn't move and Kainda remains still with Em's help.

"Go now," I say to Ninnis. "Take Nephil back to Tartarus and be free of him forever. Be free of everything. All of the darkness and—"

Ninnis laughs. "More of your forgiveness? Your mercy? It is your weakness."

"It is my strength," I say.

"You are to be pitied."

"I am stronger than you." He understands that I am not speaking about physical strength. He knows me well enough to comprehend what I'm saying.

"You know nothing of true strength," he says, standing up straight. His eyes take on a manic sheen and a thin smile spreads on his lips. It's almost like he's gone into some kind of drug induced state. "You rejected the spirit of Lord Nephil. I, on the other hand, direct it!"

Four streaks of black shoot from Ninnis's chest. When one of them strikes my chest, it's with a force comparable to Kainda's hammer. I'm thrown back into the jungle. At least my landing in the foot-deep water is cushioned. But I'm having trouble catching my breath and I've dropped Whipsnap. When I push myself up, I see that Kainda, Em and Tunis are in a similar state. In fact, Tunis seems to be unconscious, his head underwater.

I scramble to my feet and dash to Tunis, lifting his head and propping him up against a tree. It only takes a few seconds, but by the time I'm done, Kainda and Em have launched a counter attack. Em throws a volley of knifes at Ninnis, but he doesn't even move. The blackness reaches out and swats the blades from the air.

Hoping I'm not being watched, I strap on my climbing claws and take to the trees, moving quickly up into the canopy, watching the scene below as I move in.

Ninnis begins to laugh. "You are no better than that fool, Tobias."

Em screams in anger, throwing more blades as Kainda charges in. The combined attack is impressive and so refined that I think the two women have been practicing together, working on coordinated attacks the way Em and Tobias once did. Em's blades pass just over Kainda's shoulders as she runs and keeps all four black limbs busy. The attack is so well coordinated that when Kainda strikes, Ninnis has to leap back.

Kainda's hammer smashes into the lake, exploding water into the air. As she draws back to strike again, all four black limbs strike her chest and send her flying. Her hammer is knocked from her hands when she crashes into a tree and falls to the jungle floor.

Em presses her attack, but not even one of the blades gets past Ninnis's defenses. Still, they do provide a nice distraction.

When I reach the end of the canopy, I leap.

If not for the sun, my airborne attack would have been more successful, but it's not a total failure. Ninnis sees me coming at the last moment. The blackness reaches up for me, but I twist my body around and land on Ninnis's back like he's going to give me a piggy back ride. I punctuate the attack by wrapping my arms over his chest and squeezing. The serrated, triangular feeder-tooth blades slip into his flesh.

Ninnis shouts in pain and we both fall back beneath the surface of the lake. He thrashes and kicks. I can feel the blades cutting through his skin, burrowing deeper. Is he trying to kill himself? I can't imagine him panicking.

And then, he's still. Motionless.

My hands begin to sting. It grows intense, like there is acid in the water. I'm about to let go when Ninnis's body rises out of the water and takes me with it. What's strange about this is that Ninnis did not move. It's as though he levitated out of the water. When I look down and see the lake's surface beneath his feet, I know that's exactly what happened.

The sting on my hands becomes a burn and I let go.

But I don't fall. I'm caught, as though I'm in the grip of a Nephilim warrior. As I'm drawn around in front of Ninnis, I can see the blackness around my waist. The appendage undulates from Ninnis's chest, intangible, yet physical at the same time. I've seen it before. In my mind. The spirit of Nephil, but under Ninnis's direction.

The six wounds left by my climbing claws at the top of Ninnis's chest, above the darkness, ooze blood.

Purple blood.

How corrupt has he become? Could he really be so evil that he has become more Nephilim than human? Is that even possible?

The wounds stitch back together.

"No," I say.

"Yes," Ninnis says, taking delight in the word. "You're beginning to understand."

He's been toying with us. Tunis is right. He's not human. There is nothing that Em, Kainda or I can do to stop him. Not now. He's just been toying with us.

Em shouts and throws a knife.

Ninnis *allows* it to strike him, right in the eye. The wet splotch of the blade burying itself in Ninnis's face is revolting, but not nearly as bad as the slurp it makes when he pulls it out. The eyeball quickly reforms and the wound disappears. He flicks the blade aside, into the lake, as though he might a twig on a boring summer day. Then a spear of black launches out, wraps around

Em, slams her to the ground twice and tosses her to the side. She's motionless when she lands, and I hope the shallow water covering the ground softened the blow and that she's merely unconscious. But I know that if Ninnis isn't stopped, she will be dead along with the rest of us.

But I'm helpless at the moment.

Ninnis turns to me and I can see by his expression that he means to gloat. He never gets the chance. Kainda's heavy stone hammer collides with his face and throws him backwards. The blackness around my waist slips away and I'm dropped into the water.

I scramble back on shore and see Kainda hunched over, clutching her side. "Run," she says to me. "You have to live."

I ignore her, looking for Whipsnap, searching the water-filled jungle. But there is no sign of it. Not that it would help.

Ninnis roars as he floats up out of the water, held aloft by a pillar of darkness. I turn to face him, but he pays me little attention. The darkness shoots out and slams me against a tree so hard that I black out.

I come to just seconds later, but a lot has changed in those seconds. The darkness has hold of Kainda and is pinning her against a tree. My vision flickers. I hear Ninnis shouting something about betrayal and weakness.

My vision returns.

Ninnis is holding his sword, Strike, poised over Kainda's chest.

"No," I say, but my voice is weak. "Stop. Take me."

Ninnis's head slowly turns around toward me, his neck spinning further than a man's should. "Don't worry, little Solomon.

You're next."

Without looking back, he plunges the sword forward, burying it in Kainda's chest.

34

I scream. I just scream. There are no words. I'm *beyond* words. I claw at a tree, pulling myself to my feet as adrenaline surges through my body like liquid fire. Back on my feet, I see the beige staff of Whipsnap shimmering under the water just a few feet away. I step over to the weapon, bend down and pick it up. I'm moving slowly, or at least feel like I am. This could be a dream.

But I know it's not.

Water drips from the weapon as I bring it up into both hands and face Ninnis. The loud drips are all I can hear. He's watching me, his head tilted in curiosity, a sick grin on his face.

A bead of water slips to the end of the wet hair hanging in front of my eyes. When the water falls, it too, moves slowly. Impossibly slow.

What...?

A loud hiss fills the jungle. A storm has moved in.

Fast.

Faster than is natural.

Something tickles the back of my mind.

The storm... Water pours through the canopy above me, striking my skin. I feel the impact, but not the coolness of the water. Just like the river. While Kainda shivered from cold, I felt nothing but room temperature warmth. During all those hours on the wall, in the baking sun, I did not burn.

The storm!

It struck shortly after my return to the surface, tearing Clark Station 1 apart. A theory comes together like puzzle pieces. I was born at Clark Station 1 and the storm came, eventually burying the station. Years later, I returned to Clark Station 1, digging through the ice with my bare hands to find its roof. And the storm returned on the night I was kidnapped, nearly burying Clark Station 2. And when I returned to Clark Station 1 after my time in Tartarus...

The storm is a catalyst, or a sign, or something, of my connection to Antarktos! My abilities returned while the fever gripped my body and I never realized it. All this time, I could have done things differently. I could have saved Mira myself.

I could have saved Kainda.

Ninnis sees the change in me as my confidence and menace rise together. His smile fades and is replaced, for just a flash, by confusion. His body roils from inside and the smile returns. "Come, little Solomon. Die like a hunter, if that's what you believe yourself to be." He retracts the sword from Kainda's chest and her body slides down against the tree trunk, leaving a smear of red blood.

"Ninnis!" I shout and slam the mace end of Whipsnap into the water that fills the jungle. A sound like an explosion rips into the air from everywhere at once. The water all around us, for as far as I can see, bursts upwards and beads, cloaking my approach.

I splash through the wall of water and leap. The wind carries me up, covering the distance between us with ease. I swing the bladed end of Whipsnap downwards as I descend. The razor sharp blade slices even the tiniest water droplet in half as I pull it through the air.

The wall of water bursts open and I finish the strike.

Ninnis shouts in surprise, flinching back as a tendril of blackness streaks up and blocks the strike. I land on the now waterless jungle floor, willing the airborne water to strike. A powerful stream of water the size of a rhinoceros slams into Ninnis, stumbling him back. A second strike pushes him farther. The lake is behind him now.

He's rattled, but still dangerous. The blackness strikes out at me.

I leap, carried far beyond his reach, by the wind. "The land itself opposes you, Ninnis. You cannot win."

"You are nothing without it!" he shouts back, filled with anger. He hasn't had a real fight in a long time, and probably thought he never would again.

I leap to the ground, softening the fall with a burst of wind. "Then I will stop." The hovering water falls to the jungle floor once more. "Come, Ninnis," I say. "Die like a hunter."

And I mean it. I swore never to kill a human being, even Ninnis, but he has pushed me to the edge of reason this time.

The blackness retreats inside Ninnis and he takes a fighting stance with his sword, Strike. We charge at the same time, meeting with a flurry of strikes, all blocked by the other. There is no exchange of words. No taunting. This is a fight to the death and any lapse in concentration will mean a quick end to it.

After I nearly take his head off with the mace end of Whipsnap, Ninnis shouts and begins a flurry of chopping strikes that I block with Whipsnap's staff. Chips of wood fly, but the staff remains whole and I realize that when the Nephilim improved my homemade weapon, they also gave its staff a metal core.

On the fifth blocked strike, Ninnis twists his sword so that the flat end hits the staff. The tip of the flexible blade wraps around the staff and he yanks it from my hand. I'm momentarily disarmed, but he's left himself open to attack.

I kick out, hammering Ninnis's gut with a kick that would have sent any other man to the ground. Ninnis lets out an "oof!" and pitches forward, allowing me to reclaim Whipsnap, but he recovers quickly, flicking Strike to its full length and swinging it at my face.

The blade cuts a path across my vision, slicing several strands of my hair, as I tilt my head back. As I lean by body back, Ninnis fails to notice that I've also flexed Whipsnap back and before I've even righted myself, I let go of the bladed end. The weapon springs out faster than I could strike by hand and catches Ninnis across his stomach. I can tell by the tug on the blade as it passes through his flesh that is it a deep cut. A mortal wound.

Ninnis clutches his hand over the gash.

Purple blood oozes.

If only Ninnis were mortal.

Still, the wound enrages him. Had he not been able to heal, it would have been a killing blow and he knows it. I am the better hunter.

He screams and the blackness returns, shooting out toward my face.

A surge of wind carries me back and I begin to feel the exhausting effect of using my abilities in unnatural ways. Things like floating water tax me more than bending the wind toward my will. Not to mention that I'm out of practice. I won't be able to keep this up forever, and short of taking off Ninnis's head, I won't be able to kill him.

I smell blood behind me and look back. Kainda's body has paled. The sight of her fills me with renewed rage, but I don't lose control. Instead, I remember what Tobias taught me. Don't distort nature, exaggerate it. I reach out, feeling the world around me, searching for a powerful force. I find it far away and high above.

The katabatic winds, created when the colder, heavier air above the mountains, rolls down the slopes to the coast. But the winds have been tamed by the jungle. *Not for long*, I think, as I draw the cold air down faster. I can feel the air moving, but the trees resist, so I weaken the earth around them and they part like peasants before a king. The effort drops me to one knee.

Ninnis approaches, taking my undefended posture as weakness.

The darkness swirls about, agitated and eager.

He draws in a breath through gritted teeth, and raises his sword.

A crack like thunder fills the air, rising in volume. At first, he ignores it, but when the sound grows deafeningly loud, he looks up.

The jungle behind me splits open as Antarctica's most primal force—pushed faster than ever before and condensed into an area the size of a bus—surges over my head and strikes Ninnis head on. He's lifted into the air as easily as a leaf. I bend the wind upward, watching as Ninnis is carried over the lake. I push harder. Faster. Until he's just a speck. Then I let him go and momentum carries him high, and farther, hundreds of feet high and miles and miles away.

When he returns to earth, the impact will crush every bone in his body. If he falls through the jungle, it will tear him to pieces. I cannot imagine he will survive, but I will not make the mistake he did and assume he is gone forever. Something tells me I will see Ninnis again.

The effort has drained my body. I lean forward on my shaking arms, holding my head just above the waterline. I can feel consciousness slipping. But a voice brings me back.

"Sol!"

It's Em.

I turn to the voice and find Em and Tunis supporting Kainda's blood covered body. What are they doing?

"She's not dead yet," Em says, her voice desperate.

Not dead! Pain wracks my body as I fight against my exhaustion and stand up. I slosh through the water to meet them. They lower Kainda down, kneeling in the water. I fall to my knees in front of Kainda's limp body. Her tan has faded to a ghostly white. The wound is just two inches wide. It doesn't look like much, but it's just to the right of her heart. And now the organ is pumping most of her blood to places in her body where it does not belong. Even with the world's best team of surgeons, I doubt there is anything that could be done. That she has yet to die is a testament to the woman's strength, but her wounds are far beyond my ability to heal.

"She's not going to make it," I say.

Em sniffs back her tears. "Solomon, don't—"

"He's right," Tunis says. "Her wounds are too grave. Without blood of the masters, there is nothing—"

A thousand exclamations blast through my mind, but I don't take the time to utter one of them. I plunge my hands into the water, searching Kainda's waist. When I find what I'm looking for, I untie the leather thong holding it tight, with shaking hands.

"Lay her down," I say. "Under the water."

There is a moment of hesitation and I scream. "Now!"

I get the waterskin free and stand. "Get away. Move back!"

They obey, laying her back beneath the water and propping her head up on a stone. I pluck the stopper from the skin. The smell that rises from the vessel is vile, but confirms its contents. Nephilim blood collected from the shifter, Eshu, formally known as Krane. Kainda's foresight might just save her own life. Hopping out of the water and clinging to a tree, I pour the purple liquid into the water over Kainda's chest. Applying it directly to the wound would kill her even more quickly, but diluted in water, the blood will merely burn as it heals.

The purple blood clouds out around her body. But nothing happens. We wait in silence. Ten seconds. Thirty. "Should I add some more?" I ask.

"That was plenty," Tunis says. "Any more and—"

Kainda screams and sits up. She claws at the wound on her chest, feeling the pain afresh, but when the blood is wiped away, the puncture is gone, healed completely.

"Kainda," I say, leaping down from the tree.

She flinches back from me, confused. I crouch in front of her, a wide smile on my face. "Kainda, it's okay. You're okay!"

She finds my eyes and sees my smile. She glances down at the purple haze in the water, then feels her skin where the wound should be and understands.

"It's okay," I say again, and then, overcome with relief, I pull her to me and squeeze her. With her sitting and me crouching, it's an awkward embrace, but I don't care. And apparently, neither does she. She squeezes me tight, wrapping her arms around my neck and burying her face into my shoulder. The excitement of seeing Kainda alive has pushed away my exhaustion and I lift her up out of the water, giving her a proper hug. Em joins us and Kainda embraces her, too.

"Thank you," she says. "I was dead without you."

"It was you who thought to bring the blood," I say.

"I'm not talking about that," she says. "Before you. Before you…changed me. I was as dead then as I was a moment ago."

"Oh," I say. The words are kind and honest in a way I never thought I would hear Kainda say, and hearing them reassures me that no matter how powerful the Nephilim and Ninnis become, what we have here—this transforming power—will always be stronger.

35

I stop and stretch. My legs are tight from endless hours of hiking over rough terrain. Kainda stops next to me and leans against a tree. She would never admit it, but she's feeling worn down too. How could she not? We ran from the lake nearly all the way to Mount Olympus, then swam through rapids all the way back, fought Ninnis, nearly died and then spent the last two days moving back up river. But we aren't following the river this time. Nephilim have been swarming above the water, probably searching for Enki and Ninnis. Two of their three leaders are missing.

So we've taken a roundabout route, away from the river and over the craggy foothills leading up to Olympus. We've hacked through vine-laden jungle and waded through swamps. Two flocks of turkuins harassed us, but provided meals, and if not for a one hundred foot stone wall that we had to scale, we would have had to face off against a thirty-foot male cresty and its pack of nearly thirty. This wouldn't have been impossible with my abilities, but I'm still feeling the effects of my fight with Ninnis, not to mention my recent physical exertion.

But it feels good to be making progress. To be acting, rather than simply reacting. Kainda knows where Hades's quarters are inside Olympus, so that's where we're headed. From there, we'll find the Jericho Shofar. I'm hoping Hades can explain what it does. Once we have the Shofar, we'll rendezvous with the others underground and move Luca someplace safer. After healing Tunis's wounds with Eshu's blood, we sent him after the others to explain what we were doing. They'll be expecting us. And after that? I'm not sure. But at least it's a start.

Em stomps up the hill past Kainda and me. She has a crafty look in her eyes. "Look at you two, lazing around like a couple of seals."

Kainda and I look at each other as Em passes between us. Kainda gives me a smile that I've come to adore. She motions with her head to follow Em. She won't back down from the taunt, even if it was made in jest. Rest time is over.

I take a deep breath and let out a grunt. I have no trouble with being made fun of. Reminds me of my childhood. When Kainda offers me her hand, I take it and set off up the hill. I make it only two steps when a flash of pain rips through my head. I shout in agony, and fall to the ground.

Solomon.

The voice in my mind is faint, as though distant.

Solomon!

"It hurts!" I shout.

Kainda and Em are by my side in an instant.

"What's happening?" Kainda shouts.

"It's…it's…" I can't get the words out. My mind is filled with images, like I'm running through the jungle at high speed. I see Kainda and Em kneeling over my prone form. I zip past, moving a mile in a second, and see oddly shaped tree trunks ahead.

Moving tree trunks.

Legs!

Lots of them.

The Nephilim are coming!

My vision moves around, covering a lot of ground. They're everywhere. And moving among them—hunters. But are they looking for us? Or are they searching for Ninnis? It doesn't matter, either way, they're going to find us. Then, suddenly I'm moving up through the canopy. I slip through the leaves as though they don't exist and stare up into the bright blue sky that strangely doesn't hurt my eyes. But it's not a beautiful sight. It's horrible. The sky is filled with large, moving bodies. The Nephilim army has taken flight. There are more of them than I ever imagined, and they're headed out, into the world.

I'm pulled back through the canopy, past the hunters, past the Nephilim and then past myself. I move deeper into the jungle, over a fallen tree and then into a sliver into the ground. A cave.

Run!

Run, Solomon!

RUN!

The pain disappears and my mind returns to my body. I sit up fast with a deep gasp.

"Sol, what happened?" Em asks.

"Xin," I say between deep breaths. "It was Xin."

"Xin," Kainda says, her voice oozing distrust.

"No," I say, taking her arm. "He was warning me."

"Warning you?" Em says. "Of what."

I turn in the direction I saw the Nephilim approaching. "They're coming." I jump to my feet. "We have to go. Now!"

Before either can argue or question me further, I do exactly what Xin said. I run. My perfect memory guides me on the same path I took while in the dreamlike state. I see the fallen tree ahead. "This way!"

I leap over the tree and find the small opening in the ground.

"How did you know this was here?" Em asks.

"Xin showed me."

"You shouldn't trust him," Kainda says.

"He would say the same about you," I say, and then wriggle through the opening. After a momentary tight squeeze, the tunnel opens up into a cave. Em and Kainda slip in behind me and Kainda manages to yank the fallen tree over on top of the hole.

The world grows dark, but our hunter eyes quickly adjust and our other senses pick up the slack. When they do, all three of us know we are not alone in this cave. There are hushed voices further in the cave. A man and a woman. Wood smoke lingers in the air. And meat. They've cooked something recently.

These are not hunters.

I motion for the others to follow me and lead them deeper into the cave. We don't make a sound as we approach. I see the dim glowing rings of a flashlight ahead. I stop at a bend in the cave and listen.

"We need to go back," the man says. "Regroup with the others."

They're speaking English. Their accents are American.

"We'll never make it," the woman replies. "You've seen what they can do. How many of them there are. We need to find a way to stop them, here. Now."

"It's not possible," the man says. "We'd need an army."

In that moment, I know we're on the same side and decide to take a chance. I step out from behind my hiding place, hands raised and weapon-free. "I might be able to help."

The flashlight whips toward me, illuminating my body in its dull yellow glow. Despite the light in my eyes, I see the man and woman, who are dressed in black military fatigues, jump to their feet, knives at the ready. They're quick and probably skilled fighters, but I don't fear them.

That doesn't stop Kainda and Em from stepping into the light, knives and hammer out and ready for combat. I look at my two friends and say, "Put those away." They begrudgingly grant my request, most likely because they can now see that these two don't pose an immediate threat.

"What the hell?" the woman says.

"We're not going to hurt you," I say.

The man lowers his guard a little.

"Wright!" the woman shouts. "What are you doing?"

"They look like they could have killed us already if they wanted to," the man named Wright says.

"They're just kids!" she says.

"Watch it," Kainda growls.

The woman's eyes lock with Kainda's. It's like seeing two lions sizing each other up. The woman must realize her partner is correct. She lowers her knife, though she's not happy about it. "Fine."

I motion to Em and Kainda, introducing them one at a time. "This is Em. And Kainda. My name is Solomon." I reach my hand out to shake Wright's. "Solomon Vincent."

"Awfully polite for a boy in a loin cloth," the woman says.

I ignore her, as does Wright. He takes my hand with a strong shake. He motions to the woman with his head. "This is my wife, Katherine Ferrell. I'm Captain Stephen Wright, U.S. Special Forces."

"Stephen Wright?" I ask, my mind racing backwards through time and then I ask, "Junior?"

The man squints at me. "Yes. How did you—"

"I met your father once," I say, remembering Stephen Wright senior. He was a member of the expedition at Clark Station 2. He mentioned he had a son, who wanted to join the expedition, but his father kept him home. Said he thought his son would end up being killed on Antarctica. Looks like his father could be right.

"That's impossible," Wright says, letting go of my hand. "He died when I was eighteen."

I nod. "I met him twenty-three years ago." I raise my hand in a three finger salute, knowing he'll recognize it. "Scout's honor."

Wright and Ferrell look a little bit stunned.

"He mentioned you were in the boy scouts," I say.

The man leans against the stone wall and slides to a sitting position. He's clearly exhausted, possibly injured and struggling to comprehend what I'm saying.

"I met him here, on Antarctica, during the expedition to Clark Sta—"

The man's eyes light up. "What did you say your name was?"

"Solomon," I say. "Solomon Vincent."

"You're the boy!" He sits up straighter. "The boy who disappeared!"

I nod. "I was kidnapped."

"They never found you…"

"I've been here. Underground. With the Nephilim."

Wright and Ferrell both tense at the word, so I know they've encountered them.

"You know who they are?" I ask.

The man nods. "Clark explained it."

"You were with Merrill?" I say, feeling excited that I've actually met part of Dr. Clark's group.

"Do you know what happened to them?" he asks.

His question gives me my answer. "They made it, I think. Mira killed Enki. Last I saw, they were headed down river toward the sea."

Wright relaxes a little. "Enki… He's the one that nearly killed us."

"How did you get away?" I ask.

Wright nods at his wife. "Kat shot off his—I guess 'crown' is the best word for it—and he dropped us. If we hadn't fallen in the river…"

I see he's replaying the scene in his mind and I pull him back.

"Captain Wright," I say. He looks me in the eyes. "Do you understand what's happening—the war that's about to be fought?"

"I think I do," he says.

"Then you know that we'll need an army?"

"I do."

"Can you get me one?"

"Get *you* one?" Ferrell says. "I've said it before, but no one
seems to be paying attention. You're just a kid."

I ignore her and keep my eyes on Wright.

"I just need a way to call home," he says.

"*Steve*," Ferrell says.

He holds his hand up to her as if to say *don't worry, I can handle this.* He turns back to me and says "*But*, even if I could make
that call, I'm not going to until you give me a damn good reason."

I point to the canteen attached to his belt. "How are you for
water?"

He unclips the canteen and shakes it. Bone dry. I can tell he
thinks I'm going to refill his canteen from my waterskin as some
kind of peace offering, but that's not my intention at all. Not
only would it do nothing to convince him, or his wife, whose
attitude matches her name, but I tend to not do things small.

I take the canteen and step up to the wall. I place my hand
against the stone and reach out. I can feel the earth, hard and
heavy. There are pockets of air, tiny and cavernous. And there are
veins of water, flowing like blood. I focus on one of these veins
and open up a small fissure. Pressure helps me draw the water up,
though opening the stone takes more effort. But I keep the hole

small, splitting stone until it reaches the cave.

The pair remains silent when the spring opens and fresh water pours out. I could fill the canteen right there at the wall, but decide to leave no doubt that I am uniquely qualified to handle the Nephilim. I still have doubts about my ability to lead a war against these creatures that terrify me, but I seem to have a knack for vexing the monsters and foiling their plans. I don't like it and I don't feel prepared, but there is no one else.

The water transforms into steam as it exits the wall, as I coax it out. The fog fills the tunnel. I can feel it, moistening my lungs with every breath. Then I bring it in closer with a swirling breeze, condensing it over the open lid of the canteen. As though being wrung from the very air itself, water trickles from the cloud as it cyclones back into a liquid. As the canteen fills, I seal the hole in the wall with a thought. The swirling cloud disappears as the last of it converts back into water and tops off the canteen.

I screw the cap back on the canteen, give it a shake so they can hear it's full and hand the canteen back to the stunned man. Ferrell actually has her hand over her mouth.

They've been to Olympus.

They've fought the Nephilim.

But they have never seen anything like me.

I smile at them and say, "I am Solomon Ull Vincent, the first and only child born on Antarctica." I stand up feeling a sense of purpose like never before. I'm framed on either side by Em and Kainda. "I am *the last hunter*."

I look the man in the eyes. "Will you help me?"

EPILOGUE

Lieutenant Ninnis stared up at the sky. The vibrant blue looked brighter than he'd ever seen it. Birds swooped into his field of view, calling loudly, hovering on the breeze. He recognized them as seagulls, the rats of the sea. An image flashed through his mind. A boat. A voyage.

He shook his head and it was gone. A vision.

Pain filled his chest as he took a deep breath. But through the pain, he smelled salt. The ocean.

Flash.

A wedding. A beach.

Ninnis tried to scream, but only managed a hiss of air. His body, which had sailed miles through the air, had been ruined when he fell from the sky and collided with the solid, rocky coast. A little further and he would have landed at sea, where he would have likely drowned. A little more inland and he would have been hacked to pieces by the jungle trees.

But he was fortunate. His body had landed on the stony shore. Everything inside him had been obliterated. His bones. His organs. Even his mind. He'd become nothing more than a loose sack of flesh. But even now, it stitched itself back together. The pain was nearly unbearable, but he was accustomed to it.

What he could not bear were the snapshots of someone else's life replaying in his thoughts as his brain physically reformed.

Flash.

A woman. Her smile.

"Ahhh!" Ninnis found his voice as his neck came together. "What did you do to me, Solomon?"

Speaking the boy's name made it even worse. The pup had beaten him. Again. Even with the power granted him by the body and spirit of Nephil. Solomon, and his gift, had somehow been stronger.

The admission sent a wave of sickness through Ninnis's body. If he could have moved, he would have curled into a fetal position. But he was stuck in place, staring up at the sky. His hearing returned and brought the crashing of waves.

Flash!

The woman's face again. Her lips. A kiss.

Something broken inside Ninnis stitched back together, but it had nothing to do with physical repair. It was something broken long before the injuries he received today, and with the repair, came a name.

"Caroline!"

Ninnis shuddered and convulsed.

The name made him weak.

It stole his will.

His skin roiled and pulsed.

Ninnis screamed again, this time in horror.

Darkness emerged from his body, lifting him off the ground. It spun around him, forcing his body back together far quicker than the Nephilim blood could. And when he was hale again, the darkness returned, filling his body.

Consuming his mind.

Taking control.

Lieutenant Ninnis was no more.

Now, there was only Nephil.

Lord of the Nephilim.

"Solomon," the demon spoke. "You're alive."

Motion above drew his eyes back up. His brethren filled the sky like locusts, flying out to destroy the world of men. But it was not yet time.

Nephil raised Ninnis's hand to the sky and shouted, "My brothers!" His voiced boomed out over the ocean, powerful. Unnatural. But even those too far away to hear his voice, heard him in their thoughts. "Return," he told them. "Our fight here is not yet over. The boy still lives."

Nephil turned his eyes to the jungle behind him and the continent beyond it.

"Go! Find him! Bring him to me!"

ABOUT THE AUTHOR

JEREMY ROBINSON is the author of numerous novels including PULSE, INSTINCT, and THRESHOLD the first three books in his exciting Jack Sigler series, which is also the focus of and expanding series of co-authored novellas deemed the Chesspocalypse. Robinson also known as the #1 Amazon.com horror writer, Jeremy Bishop, author of THE SENTINEL and the controversial novel, TORMENT. His novels have been translated into ten languages. He lives in New Hampshire with his wife and three children.

Connect with Robinson online:
www.jeremyrobinsononline.com

COMING 2012

LAMENT

BOOK IV OF THE ANTARKTOS SAGA

TO STAY INFORMED, VISIT
WWW.JEREMYROBINSONONLINE.COM
AND SIGN UP FOR THE NEWSLETTER

CPSIA information can be obtained at www.ICGtesting.com
Printed in the USA
LVOW071415040112

262291LV00003BA/27/P